Gipsy Tales by Fred M White

Fred Merrick White was born in 1859 in West Bromwich in the Midlands of England to Joseph White and Helen Merrick who had married the previous year.

Joseph was a solicitor's managing clerk, who by the time the family moved to Hereford a few years later, had become a solicitor's article clerk.

Little is known of White's early years but what is known is that he followed in his father's footsteps and worked as a solicitor's clerk in Hereford. His father by now had also become a solicitor and times seemed quite prosperous for the family.

However in the late 1880's something went badly wrong for his father and he was imprisoned.

White had by now decided that writing was a more preferable career for him than the law. By 1891 Fred M. White, now 31 years old, was working full-time as a journalist and author, earning enough to support himself and his mother, Helen. By this time Fred's younger brother, Joseph A. White, had left home and working as a glass-blower.

In 1892, White married Clara Jane Smith. The wedding took place at King's Norton, Worcestershire, and the couple went on to have two children; Sydney Eric White (1893) and Ormond John White (1895).

As the century closed Fred's father had been released from prison and was living as a "retired solicitor", together with Helen, in Worthington in West Sussex.

By the time of the 1911 census, Fred M. White, now 52 years old, and his wife Clara were living at Uckfield, a town in the Wealden district of East Sussex. As the ominous shadows of the First World War gathered White had established himself as a popular and extremely prolific author. Indeed whether it was novels or short stories they flowed from his pen with a startling speed and many of them were initially serialized in the popular weekly and monthly magazines. His clever use of science to create imaginative and highly adventurous story lines was a particular talent of his.

During the First World War, both of his sons served as junior officers in The Royal Inniskilling Fusiliers.

The titanic struggle of the First World War and his sons' war-time experiences in it greatly influenced this phase of his writing. His novel The Seed of Empire (1916), describes early trench warfare in great and gritty detail. He went on to describe how the social changes after the war created many problems for returning soldiers as they attempted to fit back into a now peaceful society.

Fred and Clara spent their twilight years in Barnstaple in Devon, an area which also provided the backdrop for his novels The Mystery Of Crocksands, The Riddle Of The Rail, and The Shadow Of The Dead Hand.

Fred Merrick White died in Barnstaple in 1935.

Index of Contents

A MATTER OF KINDNESS

On Saturday afternoons there was peace in the Valley of Sweet Waters. Then the click and clack of pick and drill ceased, the grimy gangs went home and washed themselves, for the most part openly bewailing the fact that there were no licensed premises within five miles of the huge waterworks—works where eight thousand men were slaving and moiling to bring the glittering liquid pure across the Midlands. There was the canteen, of course, but the canteen was conducted upon narrow-minded lines, and with an abbreviated notion of the proper amount of intoxicating liquor requisite to the capacity of a self-respecting navvy. But there were ways of evading the authorities, as the said authorities sadly allowed.

The canteen was closed till dusk on Saturday, and thus eight thousand men, dotted in huts all along the lovely valley, were thrown upon their own resources. They played cricket with some vigour, they bathed in the mountain pools, there were foot races and long training walks—rambles frequently fatal to various poultry rambling thoughtlessly beyond the confines of the farmyards. Rabbits, too, were getting scarce, and Sir Myles Llangaren protested against the slaying of pheasants in August. He protested, too, against the poaching in Upper Guilt Brook, but this in a minor degree, seeing that the trout were small, albeit of excellent flavour.

As a matter of fact, three banksmen were poaching up above Guilt Bridge now. Two of them sat smoking and watching a third, who, prone on his stomach, was doing something in the stream with the aid of a stick and a fine copper wire. The thing looks impossible and absurdly insufficient, but there the captured fish lay.

"Got 'im," the fisherman grunted, lifting out a fat fish some six ounces in weight. "I dines at eight to-night in a dicky and black tie. Sort of family affair."

The other men laughed internally. The speaker was a short, powerful man, with glittering black eyes and dark snaky hair that had earned him the title of "Gipsy." The other two men were known as " Nobby " and "Dandy Dick," the latter reminiscent of an old playbill and of the fact that he usually wore a tie and had his hair with that pleasing plastered curl over the forehead which is called a Newgate fringe. Dandy also had a great, if vague, reputation for gallantry of a certain order.

As they sat there, another man came swinging up the valley. He also was of the navvy type, clean-limbed, with a suggestion of having seen service about him. He was dressed in black and wore a heavy pilot-coat, despite the heat of the day. He nodded none too familiarly.

"How do?" Gipsy shouted. The "How do?" of a navvy can be made hearty or exceedingly offensive, as the case may be. With the accent derisive on the first syllable it lends itself to quarrel in the easiest manner possible. "How do?"

The other passed on without any personal allusion to Gipsy's facial disadvantages, a fact that so astonished Nobby that he dropped his pipe and stared open-mouthed after the retreating figure.

"'Oo's'e?" he asked. "Call hisself a man! If Gipsy 'd hollered arter me like that, I'd ha' knocked his bloomin' 'ead orf. Straight."

Gipsy rolled over on his back in exquisite enjoyment. He belonged to the order of man who laughs at everything. Nobby's seriousness was a source of constant amusement to him.

"Calls hisself James Burton," he explained. "Ganger over Dandy's lot."

"It's a lie," Nobby said with emotion. "It's one of your lies, Gipsy."

"It ain't," Dandy struck in with equal politeness. "It's true. 'E's been about 'ere six weeks. Used to be a corporal in the Army, they say. No use, neither. Don't swear—can't, in fact. And when he wants anything, says 'Please. "

"Garn," Nobby said with withering contempt. "Ou'er gettin' at?"

Dandy reiterated his previous assertion, garnished with language that left no possible doubt of his absolute sincerity. Nobby had ceased to smoke for the moment. Mundane pleasures were as nothing in the contemplation of this phenomenon.

"Can't swear and says 'Please,'" he murmured. "Ow does 'e get the work done?"

"'E's after old Cocky Benwell's girl," said Gipsy, with meaning. He glanced at Dandy as he spoke. The latter winced ever so slightly.

"So I'm told," he said loftily. "But Lor'! what's the use? No chancer there."

Gipsy returned to the attack obliquely.

"I dunno," he said, with an air of profound philosophy. "Women's funny creatures. Goes in for flowers and all them things."

"Kate Benwell's very fond of flowers," said Dandy thoughtfully, "specially vi'lets. Stinking, I call 'em. 'Ad a bunch when I met 'er last night."

"Burton's got some fine vi'lets in his cottage garden," Gipsy observed. "Grows 'em under a frame in the cottage what he took from that Welshy bloke what's gone to Talgarth to live. Big blue 'uns with long storks, exactly the same as that Kate Benwell was wearin' in her boosum last night."

"I'd like to punch Burton's 'ead!" Dandy exclaimed with sudden passion.

Gipsy winked at himself with silent ecstasy. Nobby sucked at his pipe, regarding the sky with a rapt, stolid gaze. The humour of the situation was absolutely lost upon him, as the bright-eyed little man was perfectly well aware. His mental digestion was still seriously pained over the ganger who couldn't swear and said "Please" to his men.

"They'll be making me a ganger next," he said parenthetically. Nobody responded; the black-eyed man was waiting for developments.

Dandy broke out suddenly: "If a girl wants vi'lets," he said defiantly, "why, there's no reason why she shouldn't 'ave vi'lets. Come to think of it, they ain't much more offensive than bacca is to a pore bloke who can't stand smoke."

"Burton's are real beauties," said Gipsy. "Growed in a frame out o' doors where a man could 'elp himself after dark."

Dandy smiled. Gipsy's eyes conveyed nothing, though he began to see a pretty comedy opening out before his mental vision. Amusements were scarce in the Guilt Valley, and here was a fine way of adding to the gaiety of nations.

"No man could swear to a vi'let," Dandy said sententiously.

"Nor yet to a bunch of 'em, leaves an' all," Gipsy added softly. "You've got to put them all together and shove a bit of foliage round 'em."

Dandy took no heed of this original hint on the subject of floral decoration. He had gone off on his own train of thought.

"I dare say as other pore creatures up the valley—Welshies—grows vi'lets. Burton ain't got all the flowers in Wales, nor yet all the vi'lets neither. And if a man keeps them sort o' things out of doors nights, be deserves to lose 'em."

"Not as any of we 'ud take 'em," Gipsy grinned.

Nobby rose slowly, after drawing a ponderous silver watch from profound depths.

Gipsy took up his poaching apparatus again and adjusted the fine running wire.

"Just a few more," he said. "Where going, Nobby?"

"'Ome," Nobby said, with deep contempt. "It's six o'clock."

"Well, what o' that? We don't often get a chance "

"Chances be blowed!" Nobby growled. "Ain't it just six, and the canteen has been opened these ten minutes? And we wasting our time 'ere over a lot of silly trout as ain't to be named in the same day as a bloater. Come along."

This appeal, being too powerful and too cogent to be ignored, had the desired effect, and the trio made their way silently and thirstily down the valley.

II

Up to a certain time Dandy's feelings towards Miss Kate Benwell had been governed by a comfortable philosophy. He admired the girl, he had dallied with her on Sundays, but this had not prevented his liberal admiration of other women. He felt that as yet the easy swagger and the carefully oiled curl over his forehead ought not to be reserved for one of the opposite sex only.

Now things appeared to be different. That the Gipsy in his insidious way had brought about the change for his own wicked amusement. Dandy did not dream. Come what may, that poor creature of a Burton wasn't to have Cocky Benwell's girl. Besides, her eyes seemed to have grown brighter and her cheeks more ruddy of late. Critically examined, she was a prettier girl than Dandy had imagined. At the same time, she was a trifle more distant and cold than of yore. This fact landed Dandy in philosophic deeps, as it has often done in the case of cleverer men.

It was Sunday afternoon, and the valley lay bathed in the peaceful sunlight. Outside the long lanes of wooden huts, stalwart men in shirt-sleeves were minding small droves of children. Somebody was playing an accordion close by. There was a suggestion of rank tobacco-smoke on the air. Overhead a lark poured out a flood of melody. The shadow of a hawk was cast like a moving blight across the bracken.

A little further up the valley was a loose tangle of younger men. From the easy uneasiness of their attitudes they could only have been doing one thing. They were waiting for the coming of the fair, and their Sunday clothes troubled them sorely. A navvy in his working clothes is a fine sight, sometimes even an inspiring one; but the sombre raiment of the Sabbath is like a blight upon him. You can't see the magnificent torso, the knotted length of arm, the hard, lean flanks—nothing but a bunch of humanity.

Between two grinning, slouching lanes Dandy came down. He had a golf cap—plaid, with a huge purple and red star in the centre—planted at the back of his head, so that the glory of the plastered curl might not be dimmed, a handkerchief of many colours adorned his short bull neck, he had no collar, and his body was swathed in an enormous double-breasted pea-jacket many sizes too large for him. The moleskin trousers were also too long, but a pair of straps round the knees obviated that difficulty. He carried a white paper parcel in his hand.

Here was something for lambent wit to play upon. The youths ceased to chaff one another uneasily and with one accord turned upon Dandy. To flee was impossible; silent contempi would only have been accepted as a weakness.

"Carry your parcel. Dandy?" one suggested with humility. "Proud to."

Dandy turned with a smile. He was equal to the occasion.

"Couldn't do it," he said. "It's a diamond necklace for the chief engineer's wife. And you comes of a bad stock, Daniel. The last time as it was my painful dooty to give evidence agin' your old man—"

A burst of strident laughter finished the sentence. Daniel grinned redly.

"It's trotters," he said, "or pickles, or somethink of that kind. Give it a name, Dandy."

"It ain't trotters, nor cockles, nor winkles," Dandy said shortly. "It ain't the title-deeds of my new estate, and it ain't nothin' to do with nobody."

A weedy youth in an amazing check suit collapsed on the grass in a paroxysm of mirth. His comrades watched with affectionate anxiety.

"I've got it!" he gasped. "It's flowers, that's bloomin'-well what it is! A bookay with Dandy's best love to Kitty Benwell. 'Rose is red, the vi'let's blue, carnation's sweet, and so be you!' Blest if I can't sniff 'em!"

A score of more or less blunt noses were elevated in the air daintily.

"Like tripe, only more tender-like," said Daniel.

Before the roar of laughter that followed Dandy broke and fled. He was conscious of a hot, pricking sensation from head to foot. He would cheerfully have forfeited a week's wages to have preserved his secret intact. It would be many days before he heard the last of it. Many blighting retorts rose to his mind now that it was too late. He gripped the violets in his hand and shook them savagely. There was a wild impulse to hurl the offending package into Guilt Brook, but wiser counsels prevailed. The mischief was done now, and nothing could bring Nepenthe to the amused valley.

The reward came presently, however. From a bypath between the hills a girl emerged—a girl with an enormous feathered hat and plaid shawl, a girl exceedingly red in the face and black as to her eyes. Poets and painters and such effete people would have demurred to the girl's high colouring; another class of man would have summed her up as a fine woman. Dandy had made great sacrifice for her, and for the nonce in his eyes she was perfect.

"Who'd a-thought of seeing you, now?" he said breezily.

"Just what I was saying to myself, Mr. Dandy. Who, indeed?"

Dandy whistled with his eyes fixed steadily heavenwards.

"Going anywhere in particular?" he asked carelessly, yet with caution.

Miss Benwell simpered and looked down. Yet her eyes flashed alert and vigorous down the valley as if in search of somebody. She tittered. Under the circumstances she deemed it just as well to dissemble. Then

"Maybe I am and maybe Im not," she said archly.

"Well, that's just what Im going to do," Dandy observed. "So I'll walk part of the way there with you. Fond of flowers, eh?"

Miss Benwell remarked that she positively doted on flowers.

Dandy whistled again until the corners of his mouth relaxed into a broad grin.

"There's not many flowers as comes up to vi'lets," he said sententiously.

Miss Benwell agreed with enthusiasm. They were so sweet and so modest. Also she had read in the Society columns of a halfpenny novelette that they were such good taste.

"Especially blue 'uns," cried Dandy, catching her enthusiasm.

Yes, perhaps blue violets were on the whole preferable to the white variety. Their perfume was more pronounced and not too craftily subtle. All this Miss Benwell observed, averting her gaze most scrupulously from the paper parcel now getting unpleasantly warm in Dandy's powerful grip. As he stripped the paper away, the grin on his face broadened. He poked his fist rampantly under the girl's nose.

"For you," he said shortly. "A bookay. Wear 'em next your 'eart."

Miss Benwell couldn't have believed it. Anybody might have knocked her down with a feather. She placed the violets tenderly in the anatomical region suggested by Dandy.

"They are like some James Burton has," she said.

"Had," Dandy corrected. Then he recollected himself and proceeded craftily: "James Burton hasn't got any vi'lets like them. I got 'em up the valley; walked miles on purpose."

"Fancy that now!" Miss Benwell said sweetly.

"Walked my heels off almost, I did," said Dandy. "If James Burton, who's a poor creature and don't know the language—'ullo!"

The man in question stood before him. A man about his own build, with a pale, taciturn face and an eye that looked like power. His glance wandered from Dandy to the violets. His lips were parted, as if he had run far.

"You—you scoundrel!" he said. "I beg your pardon, Kate."

He turned on his heel with a slight suggestion of military salute and strode away up the valley.

Miss Benwell turned pale, flushed deep red, and tittered.

"Something disagreed with him," she laughed. "Better go this way, 'adn't we?"

Dandy gallantly replied that all ways were the same to him now. An hour or two later he returned to the huts with head erect and a sweet smile on his face. An acquaintance came down the road.

"'Ullo, Bill!" said Dandy. "So long."

"'Ullo!" the other responded. "'Ow nice you look, Vi'lets!"

Dandy stopped, clenched his fist, swore with fluency, and passed on.

III

Gipsy watched the progress of affairs from under his shrewd brows. He had engineered the whole business for his own amusement, and on the whole it was coming out beyond his most sanguine expectations. In towns Gipsy was a regular theatrical Saturday nighter, and under happier educational advantages might have blossomed into a dramatist. His first act had been eminently successful; the whole rugged community were laughing at Dandy, who, however, had his consolation in the fact that he had put Burton's nose out of joint for all time.

Still, all great victories have their drawbacks. For instance, it was by no means pleasant to be sniffed at by everybody. The boys were all whistling one air now, and on Dandy innocently asking the name, he was greeted with a chorus of "Sweet Violets." This tune he traced to Gipsy, still without suspicion of his friend's bona-fides.

"Why did you go for to do it?" he asked reproachfully.

They were all at dinner, with basins and tins between their knees. A little way off Ganger Burton was smoking in sullen silence. Though his vocabulary was mean and limited during the last day or two, there was an air about him that Dandy by no means liked.

"I never thought about you," the Gipsy said feelingly. "I was leading up to a joke. They tell me they was fine vi'lets that you gave to Kitty Benwell."

"No finer grown in the valley," Dandy responded shortly.

"And they say Burton was no end took, too, when you done him so fine." Dandy quivered. "More vi'lets where those others come from, I suppose?"

"Lots, if you go about getting them at night in the proper way."

"Then I'll show you how you can put the joke on to Burton. You go and buy a lot more of them flowers, and bring 'em down 'ere early on the ground in the mornin' afore Burton gets 'ere. Let every man stick two or three in his 'at or button-'ole, and there you are! See, old pal?"

To do him justice. Dandy "saw" immediately. The whole village bad divined exactly what was going on, and if this thing were done, every shred of ridicule would be shifted from Dandy's shoulders to those of Burton.

"Most likely drive him out of the shop," Dandy said joyfully.

"Do him brown altogether," the Gipsy responded. "If you ain't got the pluck to do it at the last minute, I'll show you a way "

"Ain't got the pluck! You see. Lor'! I'm laughing at it now."

So was the Gipsy. Only a close observer might have had a shrewd suspicion that he was laughing at his companion at the same time. Then he winked darkly and went his way.

Not one of the gang needed to be told the next morning that something was in the air. They were going to have some fun with their deservedly unpopular ganger, and that sufficed for them. Therefore when Dandy proffered all and several a few violets each next morning, the gift was accepted with a solemnity worthy of the occasion. Altogether it was a strange and moving sight, albeit correctly aesthetic.

"Not as we've any real use for them," said Dandy.

"No use at all," a big Cornishman usually called "Jigger" put in. Jigger was justly famed for his metaphors. "No more use'n side pockets to a toad."

Immediately upon this brilliant effort James Burton arrived upon the scene. He was more taciturn and deathly pale than usual. His eyes glittered strangely with the glint one sees in those of a newly-caged animal. It has been seen before now in the eyes of British troops when driven into a tight corner and orders are given to hold fire. They were the eyes of a man who was going to be dangerous when his time came. And the time was very near.

Nobody saw this save Gipsy. He began to understand that Dandy was going to get a warm quarter of an hour presently. He stripped to his grey shirt and peeled his black, powerful arms. Burton's quick gaze flashed along the slouching, smiling line of the gang. No need to tell him what had happened. Behind the anger blazing in his eyes there lurked the ghost of a smile. Mad as Burton was, he was not quite blind to the humour of the situation.

"What does all this tomfoolery mean?" he asked.

Somebody pushed the gigantic Jigger forward. He advanced with a wide, expanding smile.

"It's a sort of a club," he explained. "Don't you talk of your Primrose League no longer. This 'ere Vi'let League's the thing. It's all agin' drinkin' and swearin'—"

The speaker paused, blunderingly conscious that he had given the enemy an opening. Before he could recover himself, Burton shot in.

"I'm glad of that," he said. "Anything calculated to stop swearing will have my hearty support. You are a foul-mouthed set of blackguards, and there's a rascally thief now amongst you. And if you don't all get to work at once, I'll dock you a quarter of a day, certain."

For once Burton left off with the better of the argument. The whistle had gone and there was no time for reply. Moreover, if a man arrived a minute late, a ganger could put him back a quarter of a day, and repartee at something like threepence a word was too much like luxury.

Still, the gang could watch their leader under bent brows. He appeared to be taking less notice of them than usual, he seemed to be straining his eyes ever down the valley; he stood up erect and soldierly, like a sorely pressed outpost waiting for relief. There was more than one man in the Reserves in the gang who recognised the sergeant in that still figure.

Dandy alone was not satisfied; he shirked his work, he whistled offensively. Finally he took the stump of a cigarette from his pocket and lighted it with ostentatious care. A moment later and the cigarette was jerked into a puddle of clay, and Burton's heel upon it.

"You insolent scoundrel!" Burton said hoarsely. "I'll reckon with you presently. Move those bricks up to the head of the gully; get them done by dinner-time, or I report you for skulking. I'll teach you a lesson yet, my fine fellow!"

Dandy went limply about his task. He felt that he had a grievance against Providence. Moreover, he was properly impressed with the gleam in Burton's eye. Well, there were more violets in Burton's garden, and those violets had roots attached to them.

Where was Burton's gratitude, seeing that Dandy had thoughtfully spared a fine cluster of blooms under one of the glass lights? There was no chance of consulting Gipsy, who bent over his work in exemplary fashion.

At the first sight of real authority displayed by Burton, a moiety of the violets had disappeared. This was grovelling, and Dandy resented it accordingly. But Burton seemed to see nothing of the impression he had created, standing still and motionless, with his restless eyes strained down the valley. It was near dinner-time when a lad came up and handed an orange-coloured envelope to Burton.

He took it slowly and tore the cover. He read the lengthy telegraphic message with a blank, expressionless face, then he tore the flimsy into tiny shreds. Suddenly, without the slightest warning, he gave a yell that rang along the valley, after which he danced a hornpipe step deliriously. Before the astounded gang had grasped the situation. Burton was himself again.

"D.T.," said Jigger feelingly. There was a link between ganger and men at last. "I've seen poor beggars taken like it afore."

"It's j'y," said Gipsy, "that's what it is—j'y. And when the j'y passes away, pore old Dandy's goin' to cop a cold, see if he don't."

Burton walked through the gang unconcernedly until the whistle sounded for dinner. Then he darted vigorously down the valley, where presently a feminine figure joined him. It was only the keen eyes of Gipsy that discovered this, and amidst the babel of tongues Gipsy was strangely silent. The comedy had taken an unexpected turn, and his mind was busy scheming out a new dénouement.

IV

Dandy stalked out of the canteen at an abnormally early hour considering that it was only Monday, and consequently there was no strain on the exchequer. But there are times when the cheerful cup does not cheer, and this was one of them. In the first place, Dandy's joke at the expense of Burton had lamentably missed fire, and all the afternoon Burton had handled the men with a vigour and fire that fairly dazed them.

Again, on the way to the canteen Dandy had met Miss Benwell. On attempting to take up love's dalliance at the interesting stage where it had stopped the previous Sunday, Dandy had been met with a chilling reception. Evidently something more than violets would be needed to heal the breach. At any rate, Kate Benwell should have no more of Burton's flowers. Dandy was enough of a horticulturist to know that flowers without roots were impossible. And he was going to take his measures accordingly.

Burton's trim little cottage was in darkness. His old housekeeper was gone, and Burton was away on pleasure somewhere, perhaps at Benwell's cottage. The thought filled Dandy with melancholy. His broad chest heaved with emotion.

It was getting quiet by this time, the canteen had closed, and the long lane of lights where the huts stood was picked out here and there with increasing gaps of darkness; presently the glow of Dandy's pipe was the only light to be seen.

Then he made his way cautiously into Burton's garden. He slipped the lights from the frames where the violets grew, and tugged at the roots. It was by no means easy work, and he lacked the necessary celerity for this kind of marauding. A score of yards away stood a hut, where tools and boxes and some cases of dynamite cartridges were stored. The dynamite had no business to be there, it was contrary to all kind of regulations, but there it was. And the lock was capable of easy picking.

Dandy crept over to the hut. The lock presented no great difficulties. Locks don't as a rule to gentlemen who wear Newgate fringes and are modestly silent as to their past. Inside the hut it was dark, but by the aid of his pipe Dandy found a draining spade—a long, narrow shovel, the very thing for his work. As he stumbled, the pipe fell from Dandy's lips and disappeared under a broad ledge. To find it now without striking a light was impossible. Well, one pipe was like another, and Dandy decided to risk it. Moreover, Burton might come home at any moment.

He was getting on with his work famously. Another moment or two and the last patch of fragrant blossoms would be no more. Dandy chuckled with the air of a man who has not toiled in vain. Then a nervous grip was laid on his shoulder.

"I want you, my friend," a voice said softly. "I've been waiting for this."

Dandy rose swiftly. It was pitch dark and as yet he had not been recognised. If it came to a fight, Dandy had no clinging doubts as to his chances of success. He could knock Burton down and make assurance doubly sure by flight. The plan of campaign flashed lightning-like through his brain. Ufortunately a counter-attack flashed through Burton's brain simultaneously. As Dandy lunged for him, he stepped aside, and down went the other with a smashing blow on the jaw.

The force of the blow fairly staggered the marauder. Dandy was no novice at the game, and he realised that he had met a master. Ere he recovered from the painful surprise, he was dragged by the heels into

Burton's cottage and the door closed behind him. Every stick of furniture had been cleared from the room—it formed an ideal boxing-ring.

"Get up," Burton said pithily. "You'll take it fighting, I suppose?"

Dandy thought that on the whole he would. The sportsman would be content to give him a sound thrashing; if he shirked it, unpleasant magisterial proceedings might follow, and Dandy's feet had been too recently planted in the paths of virtue to risk that.

Taking it altogether. Dandy made a good fight of it. There was a huge swelling behind the ear, and his eyes were fast closing, also he was painfully short of breath. Finally, he lay on the floor with the haziest idea of his surroundings.

"Pretty fair for one out of training," Burton said quite cheerfully. "It's the canteen that does the mischief, my friend. Where did you get that spade from?"

"From the shed yonder," Dandy blurted out. "I picked the lock. I know you won't give a pore bloke away, but I dropped my pipe—"

"Dropped your what? Lighted?"

Dandy nodded. He was still too hazy to recollect the dynamite. With a cry. Burton dashed for the door. He stood there still as a statue for a moment.

"You madman!" he cried. "You careless, criminal fool! See what your pipe has done!"

The iron-framed windows were illuminated by a faint, unsteady glow. Down the breeze came the pungent odour of burning wood. The hut was on fire, and there was enough dynamite in it to destroy the neighbouring shanties like so many packs of cards. If the fire could be extinguished, and the cases of dynamite removed, nobody need be any the wiser, and no blame need attach to anybody.

"Come along!" Burton yelled. "There's water in the gully behind, and a couple of buckets in the kitchen. Get a move on you, and don't make any noise; if we can manage without disturbing the women and children, so much the better."

Dandy sat fettered by a sudden and all-conquering fear. Burton eyed him scornfully.

"A coward!" he said. "I didn't expect that of you."

Dandy would have protested, but his voice failed him. He was conscious of a certain grievance against Burton. He had just taken a severe punishment manfully and well, so that the accusation was in poor taste.

All the same, he was a coward. But for Burton, standing like a contemptuous sentinel in the way, he would have bolted. His idea was to have rushed yelling down the valley that a dynamite shed was on fire, and then placed a space as wide as possible between himself and the danger,

"You've got to come with me," Burton said grimly. "You cur! I'm just as frightened as yourself, only I'm not going to give way to it. I'm a soldier, an Engineer, and I know what the feeling is when the enemy are waiting for you behind cover, and you've got to advance whether you like it or not. Every man is more or less of a coward then. And if I'd given way to it, I should have been kicked out of the Army. But I didn't give way to it, and in a few weeks I shall have my commission. I came here on two months' furlough because there was a cloud hanging over me. But, thank God! my name is clear now, and the blackguard who tried to ruin me is found out. You thought I was a soft kind of fellow. I could have drilled you all. I'll drill you my lad! Come along with me. March!"

Burton spoke rapidly and clearly. There was the real ring of command in his voice; his eye was the eye of a born leader of men. Dandy obeyed mechanically. He could not have helped himself. He wondered vaguely what had come over this man. What a fool Gipsy had been!

By this time the fire had a good grip of the hut. There was water in the gully behind, and buckets. Burton threw open the door and entered. A fierce blast of heat and a pungent wrack of smoke drove him back. It would be impossible to do anything till the flames were driven back. After all, it might be necessary to rouse the people in the huts.

But not if Burton could help it. He and Dandy were working grimly now, hustling backwards and forwards with buckets, fighting the flames back inch by inch, taking their lives in their hands at the same time. As the smoke lifted sullenly, a big case of dynamite at the back was seen to burn furiously. Burton groaned to himself, his teeth close shut.

"How do you feel now?" he asked hoarsely.

Dandy wiped his streaming face. He was running wet, the beautiful Newgate curl was no more than a damp clout now. There was a queer, grey pallor under the tan of his cheeks. He laughed unsteadily.

"Funk!" he said—" blooming funk ain't no word for it. If I was by myself, I'd just 'ook it and 'owl. But I don't like to leave you."

The shamefaced Dandy would have been astounded to hear that this was courage of the highest order. But Burton's Egyptian experience had told him all about that. He patted the palsied Dandy on the back approvingly.

"We've got to get those back cases out," he said. "If we can manage those without a blow-up, the rest is plain sailing. Come along. Men have annexed the Victoria Cross for less than this."

Dandy moved forward. There was a queer choking in his throat, and he could hear his heart beating like a drum. But he was not going to be bested by Burton. They fought desperately up to the burning cases; they worked at them until their hands were covered with white blisters. But they had got them out at last. Blackened and blistered and bleeding, wet as rags from head to foot, Burton let off a jell that rang all down the valley. They had won.

"The other two—quick!" he said. "Now the water. We're safe, my lad."

A bucket or two of water and the thing was done. Dandy dropped upon a pile of clay, limp and exhausted. He was trembling like one after a long, weakening illness.

"I ain't coddin'," he said, " I ain't jokin'. Far from it. But I'm goin' to faint—me! me! Rummy, ain't it?"

'I'm goin' to faint...'

He spoke half with a sob, half with a defiant growl. Burton produced brandy and poured a little down Dandy's throat. The burly, deep-chested navvy staggered to his feet. For some little time he seemed unable to speak. "You won't give me away?" he asked. "You're a man all through, that's what you are, and I'm a fool to doubt it. But seeing as I did my best bloomin' coward or no bloomin' coward—you won't let on as I showed the white feather?"

"Rot!" said Burton. "Give me your hand."

"What for? "Dandy asked suspiciously.

"To shake, of course. Because it is the hand of a hero. My good fellow, the man who conquers fear as you did is a hero. I never saw a braver thing done, and I've seen some plucky things in my time."

"If you hadn't been here," Dandy began, "I should've 'ooked it straight."

"I say you are a hero," Burton persisted.

Dandy graciously allowed it to pass. Way up the Valley of Sweet Waters they are still inclined to make much of Dandy, but he resolutely declines to be lionised.

But for Burton he would "'a' took and 'ooked it," and to this Dandy steadily adheres. But he didn't "'ook it," and Burton was there; and this is the history of a little of the British Army.

"All right, matey," he said, "'ave your own way. So long."

"She'd never 'ave 'ad aught to do with yer, Dandy," Jigger remarked to a select circle in the canteen. "Why, she's been engaged to Burton for four years. Eddicated better'n you think. And Burton's gotten his commission. There was a lot of trouble at Salisbury over some missing stores, and Kate Benwell got 'im a job here. Women's funny things. Dandy."

"Yes," Dandy said laconically, "they be. So's men, come to that."

There was a long silence, filled by the puffing of pipes and the tilting of tankards. Gipsy lay back smoking his cigarette.

"I never could see much fun in that vi'let business of yours, Dandy," he said.

Dandy looked up suspiciously. His mind was travelhng swiftly over recent events. Then he began to discern patches of light in dark places.

"Perhaps not," he said indifferently. "Happen as you know'd something about Burton before?"

Gipsy fell into the trap.

"Old Benwell told me," he said. "Only it was a secret."

Dandy rose slowly to his feet and pointed to the door. A fine, flashing scorn was in his eye; anger filled his heart.

"If you'll come outside," he said slowly and ponderously, "just step outside for a few minutes, I'll make you as your own mother won't know you. I ain't a vindictive man—far from it—but I'd esteem the punchin' of your 'ead as real luxury."

But Gipsy was equal to the occasion. He hailed a passing potman.

"Fill all those cans," he said. "Boys, 'ere's the 'ealth of the bride and bride-groom! And if they don't make Dandy best man, they ought to be ashamed of themselves."

A LIBERAL EDUCATION

Gipsy removed his cigarette and glanced at the stranger. He was a small man, with garb reminiscent of towns—a frock-coat struggling with adversity, a glossy top-hat, owing its refulgent rays to benzoline. For the rest, the man was red, and had sanguine eyes behind glasses. He carried a big portfolio under his arm.

"If it ain't a rude question," Gipsy said blandly, "what the dickens are you after, mate?"

This was the dinner interlude. The clink of pick and the rattle of drill had ceased, and gang B14 were feeding, for the most part, out of red bandana handkerchiefs. Gipsy's cigarettes gained flavour from curiosity. Antiquarians and archaeologists he knew, but the specimen before him was quite new. He had never seen a book-agent before.

The small man, wandering into the big engineering camp high up the Valley of Sweet Waters, needed no more cordial greeting. The tiniest spark of curiosity blew up the floodgates of his loquacity. The glib words flowed on.

"'Arf time," Gipsy cut in. "The mate what shares my 'ut 'as got a parrot. Maybe as you might teach him to say a few words."

The little man smiled, nothing abashed. He spread out before Gipsy's admiring eyes a series of illustrations, views of the world at large, maps, sections of the human form divine, models of more or less up-to-date steam-engines—the whole pictorial art as applied to the "Universal Compendium Encyclopsedia," complete in twelve monthly parts at seventeen and sixpence per volume, first instalment down, the balance on faith. The book-agent is childlike and trusting, possibly because the seventeen and six down covers any predatory leaning on the part of the thirsty knowledge-seeker.

"That's what you want," said the little man, with fine insight. "This dictionary in itself, sir, is a liberal education. There's nothing—nothing that you won't find in it."

"Think so?" Gipsy asked doubtfully. "Anything about prizefights, mister?"

The little man pointed to a full-page drawing of a Roman gladiator, obviously pirated from one of the late Lord Leighton's drawings. He would like very much to know what Gipsy thought of that. The navvy was properly impressed. He regarded the gladiator's biceps critically. With a fund of knowledge like that, he would be uplifted over his fellows. Seventeen and sixpence was not much whereby he might be placed intellectually on a level with the resident engineers at Cwm House. Besides, when the thirst for knowledge played subordinate to thirst of a more commonplace character, and the exchequer was low, the volume would pawn in Rhayader for the requisite silver.

Gipsy rattled some money in his pocket. They were a sporting lot up the valley, and Gipsy's second in the Derby "sweep" had brought in a matter of over six pounds. He hesitated; seventeen and sixpence was not so much to a bachelor sharing a hut and drawing thirty-two shillings a week.

"I'll take it," he said. "And 'ere's the first money down."

"Then I'll book your order, sir," the little man said. Gipsy swelled with pride. His vivid imagination was running ahead of the present; there were reminiscences of the Industrious Apprentice in his mind.

"Perhaps your other volumes may come a little under the month, in which case—"

"Oh, I shan't mind that," Gipsy said largely. "You make out the paper."

"Certainly, sir. In that case, Form B is the one for you to sign. Your name, sir, please? Gipsy? Very good. And your Christian name, sir?"

All this with a humility that filled Gipsy with a pleased sense of importance. But as to the Christian name, there was a hitch. Did he possess one, it was lost in the backwash of boyish memories. He had never been called anything but Gipsy. At his feet lay a fine, florid drawing of Hercules. Gipsy spelt out the word slowly—his infinite resource came back to him.

"Rum thing," he said. "My Christian name's the same as that knobby bloke with the belt round his waist. H-e-r-c-u-l-e-s. Call it Herkules Gipsy, and you've got it first pop. What yer laughin' at?"

The little man explained that he wasn't laughing at all, it was merely a chronic catarrh, from which he had been a victim from boyhood. Gipsy scratched a pleasing hieroglyphic at the foot of a long, blue form, the benzoline-glossy hat was lifted with a flourish, and Gipsy was alone with the key of knowledge in his grasp—cheap at seventeen and sixpence.

The publishers of the "Universal Compendium Encyclopaedia" were less trustful than a first casual glance would have disclosed. But then Gipsy knew nothing about "remainders" or the fact that many old works of this nature—fruits of failure and bankruptcy of bygone publishers—are sold as so much waste-paper, the body or corpse being subsequently clothed in new outer garments and peddled to a confiding public through the medium of many little men with dilapidated frock-coats and hats resplendent of benzoline. As a matter of fact, had no further payment been made, the Universal Compendium Publishing Company would have lost nothing—which fact Gipsy did not grasp, as also he had no idea that he had signed a form consenting to receive the balance of the volumes monthly, or more frequently should the publisher deem the latter course expedient. Within a month the rest of the volumes did arrive, carriage paid, in a neat box, plus an invoice for something over £10, with a footnote to the effect that if the balance were not paid within fourteen days, proceedings for its recovery would be taken without further notice.

All this, however, escaped the usually sharp eye of the seeker after knowledge. It was very good of these people to send on the books which need not be paid for yet. Meanwhile, Gipsy was progressing with his liberal education. He knew something about Adam, who seemed to be mixed up in some way with a peculiar kind of fireplace; he gained some new information about Africa; of Agriculture he hoped presently to speak with authority; Algebra he was forced to ignore altogether. But the greatest delight lay in the pictures—twenty in each volume, harnessed to the text in the most indiscriminate fashion, but there they were.

It was not to be supposed that so fine a sportsman as Gipsy could have kept his new possessions a secret. There were those who scoffed, but others who firmly believed. Mothers came to know if the big book had any hints as to the teething of children, or the proper treatment of warts, whilst a third desired information as to the best way to boil cabbages; young navvies, with an eye to a hut of their own, asked Gipsy quietly if the book had any hints as to good, plain furniture, and the best way to get it on the instalment plan.

"I'm doing my best for the settlement," Gipsy replied. "It's a tough job, this 'ere liberal education, and apt to get confusing. I can't quite make out where I am sometimes. There's Anatomy. Now, is it a new kind of metal or a Colony in South Africa? But it'll all come right in time. Only I ain't found anythink about warts or furniture in the book as yet."

"Look the warts up under 'Antibilious,'" Mitchell, the painter, suggested. Mitchell was a man who had bid fair for fame as an artist at one time, only he could never keep sober for more than a week at a time. He had a fine, cynical humour of his own, a keen eye for character-study, and Gipsy, with his dramatic instincts, fairly fascinated him. "You've got the chance of becoming a great force here, old man."

Gipsy growled uneasily. He had a vague feeling that Mitchell had once been a gentleman. He was a master of phrases, too. But amongst the ten thousand navvies working, there were many who could have told lurid life-stories besides Mitchell, the painter. Dandy, standing by, sneered openly.

"What's the good on it," he asked, "when you can get Reynolds's every week for a brown? There ain't a good rattlin' bloomin' murder in all this volume what Gipsy's so set up about."

Gipsy smiled in a superior manner. Dandy eyed him with disfavour—he seemed to be on a different plane to his old mate now.

"Canteen's open," Mitchell suggested. "Come along. In the full flush of newly acquired knowledge, Gipsy ought to be able to tell us something about beer. Letter B, all in Volume I. of the Compendium."

"If you only knew what it was made of," Gipsy said in his most superior manner. All the same, he was moving towards the canteen with the rest. "There's a thing called quashyer—"

"If it was made o' mud flavoured with rotten eggs an' ditch-water," Dandy said vehemently, "it 'ud be all the same to me. Beer's beer. Been fond of it all my life, and ain't going to turn from it for all the Compendiums as was ever wrote."

A murmur of applause followed. Gipsy so far bent to popular opinion as to take a pint of the amber fluid himself. Sooth to say, he was a little tired of the Compendium. It was beginning to dawn before him that he could not live up to it. For the last month he and Dandy and Gammon had not had one poaching excursion together.

"I don't want to keep that book to myself," he said. "I'm all for public spirit. I'm going to turn it into a free library—one volume a week, turn and turn about. The subscription's a bob, limited to a 'undred. I'll collect that bob from a 'undred of you, and—"

"Bet you a tanner you don't collect five of 'em," a sportsman in the background suggested.

"Them as likes to jine, 'old up your hands," Gipsy said loftily.

There was no headstrong desire to comply with the request. The Higher Education found no favour in the camp. Two shillings only were proffered, both coupled with the suggestion that the coin should be promptly disbursed by Gipsy in the universal liquid. But even more enlightened communities have shown themselves averse to the blessings of the Free Libraries Act. Gipsy made a few scornful remarks, passed in tolerating silence.

Comparatively early the seeker after knowledge left his hut. Mitchell, the painter, accompanied him at his request. Dandy openly flouted his old ally and companion. Once the Compendium was a thing of the past, they might join forces again; meanwhile Dandy avowedly preferred the company of Gammon. It was a blow to Gipsy's pride, but he swallowed it.

Mitchell, the painter, was enjoying the comedy in his grave fashion. He had forgotten many things in his fall, but the dry humour of the born cynic had never failed him. He was laughing at Gipsy consumedly; but the latter was in bland ignorance of the fact. He jerked his thumb hospitably towards the spare chair in the hut and passed the tobacco.

"Wishing you hadn't gone in for higher classics?" Mitchell suggested.

"Got it first time," Gipsy said moodily. "It didn't sound much at first; but when I comes to think serious like over that seventeen bob a month... besides, I got all the books. And now they've sent me three papers that I can't make head or tail of. Like to see 'em?"

Mitchell nodded, and Gipsy produced three oblong sheets of dingy paper with the Eoyal Arms on the top. They were vague and depressing documents to the uninitiated, but Mitchell had had long experience in such matters during his careless days.

"What are they all about, mate?" Gipsy asked anxiously.

"County-court summons, to begin with," Mitchell explained. "According to the particulars attached to the summons, you signed an order for these books to be delivered as the publishers deemed fit. As you didn't pay on delivery, they have issued this summons—with costs, £13 9s. 4d"

Gipsy exploded into a genial laugh. The faith in his purse amused him.

"Go on!" he cried. "Me pay £13 and nine bob and fourpence. Hope they'll get it."

"Hope they will," Mitchell proceeded genially. "You took no notice, and judgment went by default."

"Sounds like a bit from the Compendium," Gipsy muttered. "Go on."

"So they issued a judgment summons, which costs you another ten shillings. As you ignored that, a committal order was made against you, as this third notice tells. Order suspended for fourteen days, but up to-morrow. You don't seem to understand, my friend. You ought to have appeared at Rhayader and explained matters to the judge. If this money isn't paid to-morrow, you will have to go to Brecon Gaol for six weeks. Why didn't you tell me before?"

"What!" Gipsy roared. "An' this a free country an' all! Lord! what a fool I've been! If I only 'ad the little cove with the slimy 'at 'ere now! Comin' along and takin' advantage of a poor, ignorant bloke like myself. An' thirteen pound nine an'—"

Gipsy paused, utterly overcome with the weight of this startling discovery. He sat in a dazed kind of way whilst Mitchell expounded the procedure of county-courts and the law as affecting the safety of the individual when the said individual had contracted a debt that he could not pay.

"If you had appeared to the summons," Mitchell said, administering what looked like very late comfort, "he might have let you off your bargain. At any rate, he would have made an order for payment at a few shillings a month, or something like that. As it is, you must pay at once. Of course, you have been the victim of a book-agent's dodge, but that doesn't help you much."

Gipsy groaned, and the flavour faded from his tobacco.

"An' all this for books!" he said scornfully—"books! Things I can't understand. I've puzzled over the things yonder till I've got a 'ead like Sunday morning. If it 'ad been for something as 'ad done me good! What shall I do about it, matey?"

Mitchell shook his head gravely. He looked deeply sympathetic. It was lucky for him that he could enjoy comedy without outward evidence of the fact. He could only suggest flight to some town. But Gipsy had cogent reasons for the peaceful seclusion of the country. He'd wait till the police came

"They're not police," Mitchell explained. "They are county-court bailiffs—probably there will be two of them, and they'll come from Rhayader. If I were you, I should go to a place where the air was more suited to your peculiar complaint."

But Gipsy declined to listen to any such temptations. His popularity counted for something. He would take a day off to-morrow and borrow the money, levying a small rate for the purpose. But, despite the measure of his popularity, Gipsy met with a cool response. The Compendium gave no play to the imagination. If Gipsy had lost a wife, for instance, or if he had assaulted a gamekeeper and was seeking to make up a tine, it would have been a different matter.

A man who wasted on classic literature hard money, that might have been spent on beer and tobacco, deserved no sympathy. A long morning's toil produced something under twenty shillings, most of it gleaned with the point of the bayonet, so to speak. In a lofty spirit, Gipsy had set out with the amiable intention of taking no more than a shilling from each man. Early in the day he had refused sevenpence in coppers with lurid language, by dinner-time he accepted a threepenny-bit from a despised teetotaller, with a wan smile. Literature is ever a thorny path.

"To think that I had come to this!" he said bitterly to Dandy in the dinner-hour. "This 'ere Joey I got from 'Anks, what's a rabid teetotaller. An' glad to get it. Well, mates?"

A gleam of the old geniality lighted Gipsy's eye as two strangers lounged up to them. There was a hard look about them; there was no sympathy in the eye of either. The taller of the two produced a paper.

"Looking for a party over a little matter of business," he said. "Name of Hercules Gipsy."

Dandy started and opened his mouth widely. Gipsy turned pale. If Dandy spoke, he was lost.

"Herkules Gipsy," the little man said thoughtfully. "Why, that's my old pal, dash my wig if 'e ain't "

Gipsy's thoughts were full of murder. His tea was hot—he thoughtfully poured about half a pint over Dandy's leg.

"What you make all that row about?" he growled. "I know who you mean, matey. It's a chap 'ere what bought a Compendium from a little bloke with a shiny 'at. If I'd got 'im 'ere—leastways, I—well, there! Gipsy told me all about it last night."

"Are you come to arrest 'im?" Dandy asked with sudden inspiration.

"For debt," the big stranger explained curtly. "Non-payment of a debt on county-court judgment."

"Seen 'im lately?" Gipsy asked carelessly and perspiringly.

"Seen 'im this mornin'," Dandy replied. "Got all his best on, and his other things done up in a 'ankerchief . 'Goin' to North Pole?' I says. ''Ookin' it,' says he. 'What for?' says I. 'Got into a bit of a mess,' says 'e. So I let 'im go, and there's an end on it."

"Unpopular, surly sort o' bloke, he was," Gipsy said thoughtfully. "Never did nothing but poke about in readin' books or that kind o' thing. Bet a tanner 'e's gone to Rhayader to look after 'is wife."

Dandy volunteered further details. Hercules Gipsy owed him a lot of money—he owed money all round, in fact. Dandy was glad that he had got into trouble. The strangers moved on presently and were lost to sight down the valley. Gipsy sat on a stone and wiped his beaded forehead.

"I owe you one for that, mate," he said. "But those chaps'll come back again. It mayn't be to-day, or yet to-morrow, but they'll come. And what's the good o' this?"

Gipsy displayed a big fist with some poundsworth of dingy silver in the centre of the hard palm, and snarled at it with bitter contempt. Dandy smiled. For the middle of the week this was wealth.

"I pulled you out of that, old 'un," he said. "An' a man don't think fast on a 'ot day like this. Might as well be 'ung for a sheep as a lamb."

"Righto," Gipsy said recklessly. "Come on. This way to the waxworks. It's going to be sixes."

The canteen stood invitingly open, the day was hot. The full measure of the canteen allowance was partaken of, and then the pair slipped out of the Settlement to the inviting shade of a public-house opposite. As Gipsy's pocket grew lighter, his spirits rose.

"I'll go and lie down," he said hazily. "I've got a plan. Dandy. I've got a plan, if I could only think of it. It's a very good plan, mate. I'll raise the money and pay off the little bloke in the glossy 'at. No, I won't, I'll keep the brass and see him further first!"

He pulled his cap fiercely over his eyes and strode resolutely in the direction of his hut. Dandy sighed into his empty mug and followed with discreet silence.

For the time being the philosophical side of Gipsy's nature was submerged. He had expected better things of his fellow-men. Also there was the blow to his pride. He had yet to learn that when popularity pulls against pocket, the struggle is a terribly unequal one. Anyway, this money must be found. Gipsy had tried to raise the rate openly and upon the strength of his individuality, and he had failed. He had no intention of going to gaol—his Romany blood turned cold at the mere suggestion; he would resort to strategy.

The man was a born dramatist and a maker of stories, only a beneficent legislation had not caught him early enough to teach him the proper equipment. He approached the matter now from the point of view of the novelist who has got his hero in a tight place and is bound to get him out of it again.

As Gipsy sat over his pipe, illumination came to him. He must impose upon a credulous public. A wide grin expanded over his face. He took down the volumes of the Compendium and selected a dozen or more of the engravings therein, and then by the aid of his knife he detached them neatly from the bindings. The plan of campaign was perfect. Gipsy waited now to see Mitchell, the painter, who took his evening stroll about this time. Presently the artist lounged along.

"'Arf a mo'," Gipsy drawled. "Want to earn a quid?"

Mitchell shook his head doubtfully. As a rule, his elderly housekeeper drew his pay and allowed him a certain modicum for tobacco-money. It was the only way in which the artist could possibly wrestle successfully with the drink craze. Give him a sovereign, and he would do nothing till it was gone.

"How long have you been a capitalist?" he asked. "Left over from the library, eh?"

Gipsy said something forcible on the subject of tabloid education. He pointed to the selected engravings taken by him from the Compendium.

"What a fool thing to do!" Mitchell expostulated. "Poor as the volumes were before, they are worth nothing now. You have utterly spoilt them."

Gipsy winked solemnly. There was all the air of a successful dramatist about him.

"I'm going to get you to help me," he said. "You just go and get those paints of yours—the oils. Bring all the pretty 'uns. I've got to get out of this mess; and if I ain't just a bloomin' Bobs at this game, strike me pink! Look at this bloke."

At arm's length Gipsy held up a counterfeit presentment of Hercules in a boxing attitude. He stood on a pedestal and was obviously "after" some celebrated statue or another. Gipsy eyed the muscular form admiringly.

"That's a model of physical development," Gipsy remarked. "The blighted Compendium says so. Also it's a work of art. Just so. An' if I took and tried to raise a bob on old 'Erkules in the canteen, I couldn't do it. But nobody's seen 'Erkules, which is a good thing. He's no good now, but you'll see when we've done with 'im. Go and get your paints."

There was comedy here somewhere, as Mitchell recognised. He had a profound admiration for Gipsy and his many "slim" expedients. He came from the class of men who know how to jest with a straight face. Mitchell came back presently with his oils and brushes, and Gipsy carefully locked the door before lighting the lamp.

"Now look 'ere," he said. "You've got to 'elp me over this job, matey. We've got to raise the spondulix from the delooded public. You just tackle old 'Erkules as I tell you. Take and paint 'im in tights, and a championship belt round 'is middle. Shove them bunches of fives of 'isn into four-ounce gloves."

"Make him a boxer and a bruiser up to date?" Mitchell asked with a grin.

"That's the time o' day," Gipsy said drily. "Up to date. Turn that 'ere butcher's block what he's standing on into a platform, and a rope round it. Wade in."

Mitchell waded in accordingly. At the end of half-an-hour the classic engraving of the famous athlete was transformed into a glaring oil presentment of a modern boxer of the approved type. Mitchell had been purposely prodigal of his colouring, and Gipsy was loudly enthusiastic. The flagrant vulgarity of it appealed to him strongly.

"Spiffin'!" he said. "Just the ticket for soup. All it wants now is a nice 'omely flavour of the pub about it. Just stick a red triangle with 'Bass's Beer Only' underneath, just behind old 'Erkules's 'ead, and there you are. What!"

Gipsy stood back and surveyed the work critically. Its crude colouring and flaring vulgarity touched him to the soul. No British "navvy " with a grain of sport in him could look upon that picture without the longing for possession.

"How long before it's dry?" he asked.

"Dry now," Mitchell explained. "That porous paper soaks up the oil directly. This is my masterpiece, Gipsy. I never hoped to paint anything like that."

Gipsy nodded approvingly. He was in the presence of genius. He took the picture up and rolled it with the greatest care. He was going out, he explained, as far as the canteen. If the painter possessed the fund of humour that Gipsy credited him with, that virtue would be gratified if Mitchell would look into the canteen a little later.

The canteen was pretty full as Gipsy entered. He took up his place at an empty table and spread out his work of art before him; he appeared to be in rapt and admiring contemplation. Presently one or two of his own gang lounged across, to see the cause of this thoughtful silence. They fell under the spell of Mitchell's genius.

"What is it, Gipsy?" asked one in an awed voice. "Where did you get 'im from?"

"Won 'im," Gipsy said carelessly, "in a raffle. A bob a share—last time I was in Cardiff. O' course you know who that is?"

"Bloke just trained ready for a mill, I reckon."

"Bloke ready for a mill!" Gipsy said, with bitter scorn. "Where do you come from? Was it four or five years you got? That there's Tom Flannigan, the Irish Terror, just before his successful scrap last March with Long Coffin, the American Champion. Knocked 'is man out after thirty-two rounds, lasting two hours."

'That there's Tom Flannigan, the Irish Terror.'

The others gasped. The famous fight was still fresh in the recollection of most of them. It was impossible to look upon that form and those colours unmoved. Gipsy pinned the picture to the matchboarded wall behind him, and the hands crowded round to admire. No famous creation from a fashionable artist hung on the line attracted such respectful attention.

"I've got others," Gipsy said. "I value 'em at eight 'undred pounds. There was ten thousand put into that raffle, at a bob a nob, and I got first prize. Came by parcel post to-day, they did. Make me wish I was a married man, it does. To think of a 'ut, with some good sticks o' furniture, and them things 'angin' on the walls!"

"Want to sell it, Gipsy?" a distant voice asked anxiously.

Gipsy looked up, caught the eye of Mitchell, who was standing in the doorway. Neither man smiled; but if both had shouted with laughter, they could not have understood one another more perfectly. The luxury of the comedy was theirs alone.

"Well, I wasn't thinking about it," Gipsy said slowly. The suggestion appeared to give him a fresh train of thought. "It ain't often as a poor bloke like myself gets a picture what lots of nobs would be proud to 'ang in their drorin'-rooms. But I've 'ad misfortunes, as most of you know, and a few pounds—what'll you stand, Jimmie?"

"Ten bob," Jimmie said promptly, "an' a go of gin."

Gipsy snorted. If it had been pounds, now! He stood up, as if inspired by a new idea. The full light of the lamps shone on the dazzling colour picture. Why not raffle it at a shilling a share? Say sixty shares at that modest figure. A responsive murmur followed. Half-an-hour later, Gipsy strolled thoughtfully homeward with a bulging pocketful of greasy silver coins. Mitchell followed. After all, there were other acts to follow, and the first had been excellent.

"You'll get on," the painter said. "I should never have thought of that."

"Came to me like a perspiration," Gipsy said modestly. "Only I might 'ave waited a little longer. Believe I could 'a' got the whole bloomin' thirteen quid out o' that 'ere effort o' yourn. But there's more where the other came from. 'Oo's this?"

"That is a portrait of Sarah Siddons, the great tragedy actress, after Romney," Mitchell explained, as Gipsy proffered him a further illustration from the Compendium. "What do you propose to do with her? Leave us some of our illusions, Gipsy."

"She'll do," Gipsy muttered. "She's going to be the cellubrated Miss Netta Montgomery, what played in Nelson's portable theatre down at Cwm all last winter. Every single bloke in the settlement was fair gone on her, though I found 'er second-class myself. Lot o' yaller 'air an' a dress all over spangles. You know the sort of thing. Then I'll get another three quid for that. 'Ere's a cottage and what you call a landscape."

"Anne Hathaway's cottage," Mitchell murmured.

"Niver 'eard of 'er," Gipsy went on. "But it's goin' to be made into the Red 'Ouse up the valley, where the shepherd killed his wife in the spring. Put a few piles o' timber and a derrick in the background, and there you are. I shan't do much with it amongst the boys, but the wives will fairly rise to it. Give 'em a touch of the 'orrors, and you've got 'em every time."

Mitchell nodded. His face was grave, but his eyes danced with amusement. The oil was burning low in the lamp before he had finished his work. There was an expression of placid contentment on Gipsy's face.

"Come in to-morrow and do the other one," he suggested. "Strike me! I shan't want to trouble you any more after that. 'Picture of the Bronze 'Orse at Venice.' Touch 'im up, and put a boy in a pair o' tight breeches leadin' 'im by a 'alter, and there's the winner of the year's Derby what most of us backed. I'm goin' to pay for the bloomin' Compendium on this job, so as it'll cost me nothink. So long."

The following evening was a busy one for Gipsy. As he had confidently expected, there was a brisk demand amongst the younger fraternity over the portrait of Miss Netta Montgomery. She fell to Gammon, who had been a particular victim to her charms, but not until Gipsy had disposed of nearly eighty tickets. An almost equal popularity was enjoyed by the transformed Bronze Horse, whilst the mothers of the camp took a vivid, if morbid, interest in the picture of the Red House, where the murder had been committed.

Gipsy raked the money in and posed as a benefactor at the same time. His enterprise and public spirit enabled the settlement to gratify a natural passion for the best in art. But for Gipsy these elevating objects would never have found their way here at all. Later on, in the seclusion of his hut, Gipsy counted his spoils.

"'Ave some baccy," he suggested hospitably to Mitchell. "Fill your pouch... Fourteen pounds seventeen and sixpence. Dunnow where the tanner came from. When the bailiffs come, I shall be able to talk to 'em now. Still—"

Gipsy's face clouded thoughtfully. He had earned all that his own bright and particular seemed a pity to waste it on mere publishers. Many a beautiful spree, many a lurid Saturday night shone from that pile of silver on the table.

"Seems a pity, don't it?" Mitchell suggested, watching his companion's thoughts.

"Pity!" Gipsy snorted. "It's what them drapers call an appallin' sacrifice. Still, it ain't me what's goin' to pay for the Compendium. An' yet—"

Gipsy pulled at his pipe thoughtfully. He sat there under the lamplight after Mitchell had departed, thinking the matter out. The novelist in the rough had got his hero out of a tight place; but in all properly appointed romances the hero not only escapes from imminent peril in the deadly breach, but is in honour bound to score over the miscreants who, for the time being, have triumphed. And Gipsy practically had not scored at all. Being his own hero, he felt it. Thoughtfully he took an envelope and addressed it to the publishers of the Compendium. Then he produced a sheet of paper and laboriously proceeded to write a letter. It was a slow and painful process, but in the end it seemed satisfactory :—

Box 171, P.O.
Water Company's Scheme,
Cwm Valley.

Sirs,

A few friends of Mr Ercules Gipsy wot's left the valley and no address is desirous of seein wot I can do in the matter of the Compendium. Which never ought to have been sent in the way it was. Out of respec to the memory of Mr Gipsy and if he could be allode to come back we'll between us send you four pound ["five" scratched carefully out] and no questions ask. This to clear off all back pay and put the time sheet right. A answer from you by the next post saying as this is all right money will be sent.

Yours respeckfully for 6 of us,

Jon Price.

Gipsy duly despatched his letter, comfortable with the assurance that there were some scores of John Prices in the settlement. For the next day or two he was dreamy and preoccupied. The third day brought a letter from the publishers of the Compendium, offering, with large magnanimity, to cancel the debt and all proceedings on receipt of five pounds, coupled with a rider to the effect that the money must be received by return of post. It cost Gipsy a pang to part with his five sovereigns, but there was sweet consolation in the fact that he had the Compendium, plus nearly ten pounds, and that without the outlay of a single penny of his own money. Thus do the heroes of romances score over mere mundane and less brilliant creatures.

Gipsy ran into the arms of Mitchell as he came from the post-office.

"Suppose you had to pay?" he asked.

"Suppose I didn't," Gipsy said thoughtfully. "I wrote a letter to the Compendium bloke sayin' as a few pals of Gipsy's 'ud like to—what you call it?—compromise. And they took five bloomin' quid. And I've just posted the brass. What do you think of that?"

Mitchell shook his head admiringly and passed on. Gipsy returned thoughtfully to his hut. The gay volumes of the Compendium seemed to smile down at him. He could think with toleration of the words of the wily little book-agent now.

"After all," he muttered—"after all, there's something in a liberal education."

A STRANGER IN BOHEMIA

The little man with the snaky hair and deep-set eyes, sitting in the corner of the canteen, was known to all and sundry as "Gipsy." To the uninitiated this title, of course, had no geographical significance. To the casual, Gipsy was no more than a foreman ganger employed upon the great new water system at Penguilt; but there were men working there who could have told you that, in the freemasonry of the craft, the name of Gipsy carried from the Golden Gate to the Yukon Valley, and from the Nile to the Amazon. The little man sitting there, drinking his beer and smoking something particularly painful in the way of a cigarette, was Bohemian to his blunt finger-tips. He would have resented the suggestion that he was anything but an Englishman, though his looks belied him, and the Zingari in his blood drifted him from time to time all over the world. He was a master of argot in many languages; he had its slang and its illusive profanities on the tip of his tongue. Wherever the spade and the drill and the dynamite cartridge carried in the making of the world's highways, you could have put Gipsy down over a gang of men, be they white or black, orange or copper-coloured, and he would have handled them, too, and they would have known that they had a man over them from the word "Go!"

Gipsy, therefore, was a celebrity in his way. Great captains of industry knew him by name; they encountered him from China to Peru, so that he formed the link between East and West, and in a way was proud of it. Gipsy might have made money had he been less generous and not quite so romantic. For there was a strong vein of sentiment in the little man, who, had he been blessed with the advantage of education, would most assuredly have made a name for himself as a dramatist. He was a Sardou without power of expression, a Shakespeare in embryo, lacking the gift of the written word. As a matter of fact, he could hardly write his own name; but he could plot and plan, and many a comedy had been played in the Settlement which had not been rehearsed from the written scrip.

There was nothing that Gipsy liked better than the weaving of romances in which he played the leading part. And to his credit, be it said, most of them were founded upon fact. There were those amongst the tough brotherhood of the pick and shovel who implicitly believed all that Gipsy said, and on the other hand were ranged the cynical, who spoke of him frankly and luridly as a liar. But this is essentially a penalty of greatness, and touched Gipsy not at all. In one respect, however, even the most doubting regarded Gipsy with veneration: he was by far the most gifted and accomplished poacher amongst the ten thousand odd gathered together there amongst the mighty reservoirs carved out of the hillsides of Penguilt. Everybody knew this, and Gipsy was flattered accordingly. There were trout and salmon there, partridges and pheasants, and grouse, too, on the upper moors. Gipsy looked after himself all right, and the mess-mates in his hut, but to the rest of them he was profoundly and almost eccentrically modest.

He talked fast enough—in fact, he was always talking—but not about the best way to circumvent the wily salmon or the elusive trout, and the more silent Gipsy was on these points, the more sure were his satellites when he was planning some wily campaign on his lordship's preserves. He was talking now, telling one of his stories in which he was playing the hero, as usual. It was hard on the time when Gipsy usually embarked upon his third pint of beer, and his mood had reached the softened and sentimental stage.

"I am tellin' you no word of a lie, mates," he said. "There is a poet as I once 'eard on as said somethin' about flowers what was meant to blush unseen. I read that bit in a paper as come my way about fifteen year ago, when we was makin' that dam for the Russian Government out in Manchuria. Remember it, Joe?"

The man addressed as Joe nodded over his pipe. One of the beauties of Gipsy's stories was their verisimilitude. He rarely embarked upon a romance without the presence of some witness who could speak geographically. Therefore Joe nodded.

"I made a tidy bit o' money them times," Gipsy went on. "I couldn't well spend it, and it began to pile up, till I'd sent 'ome nigh on seven 'undred quid in about three year. And then I begins to ask myself what I should do with it. Not but what I'd got an idea in me 'ead. Fust-rate idea for a play it were, too. It was all about a gel—a little gel as I picked up on them plains of Manchuria. She wasn't nothin' more than a peasant's kid as 'ad been abandoned by 'er father and mother in consequence of a bit of a scrap what 'ad taken place between some Manchus and a tribe of Chinese pirates. Found 'er in a burnin' 'ut, I did, wrapped up in a bit o' blanket. Funny thing, but that kid took to me from the first. And blowed if I 'adn't got my 'eroin' fust 'and!"

"Lor, what a liar it is!" an admiring voice came from the background. "But go on, Gipsy, cough it up."

"I was about to do so," Gipsy said, with some dignity. "And if you don't believe as that scrap took place, ask ole Joe 'ere."

Joe gave the desired assurance, and Gipsy resumed.

"As I was a-sayin'," he went on, "there was my 'eroin' all ready-made. What did I do with 'er? Why, adopted 'er, of course! I 'ad to put off the play, but that didn't matter. Now, mind, I'd got a tidy bit o' money put by, which I was pretty certain to do in fust time we got back to England.

So I goes to one of our engineers what 'ad got a missus and kids out yonder, and I puts it afore 'im plain. I tells 'im as that little nipper, what might 'ave been about four year old, was goin' to be my heiress."

A burst of laughter followed, but Gipsy went on gravely.

"I wanted that kid sent over to England to eddicate. And our engineer 'e says: 'Good iron!' Says that I should only make a fool of meself if I kept the money. So I passes it all over to 'im, and 'e agrees to spend it at the rate of about a 'undred quid a year on the kiddie's eddication, and, what's more, 'e does it. Now she is a lady, a real proper lady, as swanks about in 'er silks and satins, and mixes regular with the nobs. Fit to go into any 'ouse in the kingdom, she is. They tells me at the present time as she's governess to the daughters of a bloomin' earl. Lives in the 'ouse with them, and is regular one of the family. She's dark and she's beautiful and she's 'aughty, and I ain't sure as a lot more earls ain't on their bended knees askin' 'er to marry them."

"Ain't 'e a knock-out?" a voice in the tobacco fog said, appealing. "Ain't 'e better than a Sunday piper? Ever stay with 'er, Gipsy? Ever put in a week-end at one of them castles?"

"We 'ave never met," Gipsy said loftily. "My adopted daughter 'as not seen 'er toil-worn parent. Probably she never will. Who am I that I should stand in the girl's way? Why should I drag 'er down to my sordid level? It's what some newspapers call a perlite fiction that I am dead, and that in future the beautiful orphan will 'ave to rely upon 'erself for 'er daily bread."

"She might be able to lend yer a bit," a practical member of the audience suggested. "If she gets spliced to one o' them dooks you spoke of, she ought to be good for a couple o' quid a week. But it's all lies! We are a set o' fools to listen to it all. And yet, when you begins to tell one o' these 'ere stories o' yours, I am never quite sure whether you are a blithering liar or not!"

Gipsy smiled with the air of a man who is the recipient of some graceful and well-chosen compliment. He knew that he was holding his audience in spite of themselves, and these cynical lapses into common-sense were really attributes to his powers. One man, a little less easily moved than the rest, jeered openly.

"Wery good," he said. "But yer story don't go far enough, mate. There's few chaps in this camp what knows the Surrey Theatre and the old Britannia better'n me. I've seen that 'eroin' o' yours 'undreds o' times. Why, you're the bloke as she finds dying in a work'ouse, or drags into the marble 'alls by the scruff o' the neck on a snowy Christmas Eve! She calls you 'er benefactor, and 'er husband, the dook, shakes you by the 'and and fills you up with port wine and roast goose. So far it's all right, Gipsy. But you've got to 'ave somethin' as proves your indemnity."

"That proves my what?" Gipsy asked. "Lor, what an ignorant set o' blokes you are! Meanin' my identity, I suppose?"

"Well, that's just wot I said," replied the other man diplomatically. "You've got to 'ave a mark o' some sort—a wound as you got when you rescued 'er from the fire, or perhaps a photograph."

Gipsy smiled in a superior fashion.

"I thanks the right honerable gentleman for makin' the remark," he said. "He's been good enough to call me a liar. Well, I can't show no wounds—that's wot they calls scars in the play—but the photograph's all right. 'Ere, wot price this?"

From a capacious inner pocket Gipsy produced a stiff leather case, from which he took a framed photograph. It represented a girl on the eve of womanhood, a tall dark girl in evening-dress, with a face serenely beautiful and faintly smiling. She seemed typically one of the upper classes, essentially to the manner born, with that elusive suggestion of superiority that makes the thing which, for want of a better word, they call a lady. For a moment Gipsy regarded it with a certain reverent affection. Grudgingly he released it from his horny thumb and forefinger and passed it round amongst his mates.

"There yer are," he said defiantly, "that's the lidy. And if anybody 'ere calls 'er anythin' else, I'll push his fice in!"

There was no occasion for the threat, for the spirit of cynicism had vanished the moment that Gipsy had crowned his story with this startling piece of circumstantial evidence. Even the man in the far corner was silent and almost inclined to believe.

"Where's the lidy now?" a respectful voice asked.

"I dunno," Gipsy said shortly. "I got this photograph about two years ago, and I ain't made no inquiries since. I ain't goin' to stand in the girl's way. Some of these days there'll be a duchess or a countess as'll never know as she owes 'er 'appiness to a common ole bloke named Gipsy."

With these dignified words, Gipsy collected his photograph and walked slowly and sorrowfully out into the darkness. He conveyed a subtle impression that deep and tender chords had been touched, that he was a strong, silent man who wished to hide the full measure of his grief from the eyes of a cold and unsympathetic world.

As a matter of fact, this dramatic exit was a skilful ruse, born of the knowledge that Gipsy was going up over the far side of his lordship's preserves in search of a casual pheasant for the benefit of a sick friend. His gun was concealed in the leg of his corduroy trousers, and he carried half a dozen cartridges in his waistcoat pocket. He was not out to-night on a grand scale—he merely wanted a brace of pheasants for the pot, and an odd bird or two for the wife of a ganger down at Coomlyn. Therefore it behoved him to be careful. He knew that the keepers were out in force, and the fact that they had marked him down as a dangerous poacher added zest to the expedition. Gipsy had poached game of all sorts in many lands, but never yet had that wily Bohemian been laid by the heels.

It was the one thing he dreaded, the thing he was horribly afraid of. For the sun on the hillside, the breeze in the trees, and the smell of the mouldy woods, were just the breath of life to this son of Zingari. He was as strong as a bull and as tough as leather, and impervious to pain, and yet three months in gaol would have been the death of him. He would have pined and died, as an eagle droops in a cage. The mere thought of captivity gripped him by the heart and caused his footsteps to falter; but the call of the wild was too strong, and the unseen force dragged him on till he stood ankle-deep in the fallen leaves and saw the pheasants roosting overhead.

All his prudence had gone to the winds now; he raised his gun, and two of the birds dropped like gorgeous stones at his feet. And at once the dank and dripping wood became alive with men. Gipsy asked no questions—he was hardly taken by surprise. He dropped to his knees and hid his gun cunningly. Then he was on his feet again, flying headlong downhill for dear life. It was not for him to show fight, for Gipsy was no lover of violence. He was a poacher pure and simple, and all he wanted now was to obliterate his tracks and make his way to freedom. He knew every inch of the ground—no woodman born on the estate knew the covers better than he—for to him woodcraft was an instinct, and it had come to him with the first breath of life.

He saw the enemy spread out like a fan, he saw the long-legged head-keeper working round to the right to cut off his retreat. There was only one thing for it, therefore, and that was to break through the big spinny, through a wide belt of shrubs, and thence make a bold dash across the lawns in front of Lord

Llanwye's house. It was a counsel of despair, a forlorn hope, but Gipsy did not hesitate. He ran on and on until his legs began to fail him and his heart beat like a muffled drum. He was in sight of the house now, the long, low house all in darkness save for the light glowing in the drawing-room windows. Self-consciously, Gipsy could see that one of the drawing-room windows was open to the lawn, though the blind was drawn down, and almost at the same moment he could make out the lean form of the head-keeper lurking in the shadows at the far end of the terrace.

For once in his life Gipsy knew the meaning of the word "fear." It was not that he was physically afraid. But his imagination was at work, and he could see himself within the four walls of a prison cell, pining for the open fields and the smell of the good red earth. He was utterly spent for the moment, he knew that he would be like ripe corn for the sickle of the long-legged keeper, and a certain sense of desperation seized him. He did not even stop to think; he crept across the terrace and, lifting the blind, walked straight into the drawing-room of Llanwye Castle. Here was melodrama all ready and glowing to Gipsy's hand.

He dropped the blind and looked around him with an admiring contemplation of the finest stage-setting he had ever seen. Here was a magnificent room filled with pictures and flowers and gleaming statuary, here were thick, luxurious carpets, and everything blended into one harmonious whole under the half-dim light of the shaded electrics. Never in his life had Gipsy imagined anything like this, never in his wildest flights of imagination had he conjured up so fair a scene. He had got himself in hand now; he was ready for the part that Fate had thrown in his way.

For the moment, at any rate, he was the leading character on this bewildering stage. He was the actor-manager who cannot sustain a whole drama by himself, and Gipsy began to look round vaguely for something in the way of a heroine. Therefore there was no surprise in his mind as he saw her arise from a big ingle-nook and come slowly and majestically in his direction. She was young and tall and willowy, as every properly constituted heroine should be; she was serene and haughty and absolutely self-possessed. She seemed part and parcel of that room, she was one to the manner born, a true patrician who had evidently drifted down the primrose path of life in silk attire and with the world for slave at her dainty feet. She was not in the least annoyed or angry or even surprised. She was just a specimen of glorious womanhood, as far above Gipsy as the star is above the moth. He stood there open-mouthed, drinking in her glorious beauty, as yet unable to grasp the situation and fumbling for his cue. It was up to her to speak first, of course; she had possession of the stage, and he waited for her to begin.

She looked at him as if he had been some strange animal, some annoying insect, a kind of human wasp to be driven out unmercifully. And then it came to Gipsy like a flash.

"What are you doing here?" the girl asked.

"Well, I was out poachin', miss," he explained. "They got me into a tight place, and so I just run in 'ere like a frightened rabbit. After 'is lordship's pheasants, I was. You won't give me away, miss. I couldn't go to gaol, miss; it 'ud be the death of me. And I never did no real 'arm to anybody. Besides, if I don't make a mistake, I am an old friend of yours."

The tall, slim figure standing there stiffened, a look of cold displeasure came into the dark eyes.

"I think you are mistaken," the girl said. "My name is Trevelyan—Hilda Trevelyan. I am governess to Lord Llanwye's children, and for the moment am in charge of the house. And I am quite sure that I have never seen you before."

By way of reply, Gipsy dived into his pocket and produced his precious photograph. Without a word he handed it over to his companion, who looked at it long and narrowly. It seemed to Gipsy that she was breathing a little faster, and that the full red of her lips had lost a little of their colour. But she gave no outward sign save that her dark eyes were fixed steadily on Gipsy's face as if she were trying to read his story.

"Where did you get this?" she said. "Tell me the truth."

"Would I tell a lidy like you a lie?" Gipsy retorted. "I've been all over the world, and I don't deny as I made a good bit o' money now and again. But I never could keep it, 'cause I ain't that sort. And that's why I've got nothing in the world as I values except the photo in that lily-white 'and of yours. It was give to me by a gentleman what was called Mr. Masters. An engineer, 'e was—one of my bosses in a job we 'ad years ago in Manchuria. Now I dare say you may 'ave 'eard of this?"

"You are speaking of my guardian," the girl said coldly. "To all practical purposes, Mr. Masters was my father."

"You don't mean to say 'e is dead, miss?" Gipsy said.

"He died a few years ago. Both he and his family were killed in China during the revolution there. It seems a very strange thing that I should be standing here discussing my most intimate affairs with a common poacher and a man I have never heard of before. If you have any intention of blackmailing me—"

Gipsy thrilled. The drama was going splendidly, for here he was in the centre of a most glorious stage, playing lead to the most exquisite of heroines, and she was actually accusing him of blackmail. The woods and the pheasants were forgotten now; the lurking foe outside ceased to exist.

"You touched me on me tenderest point," Gipsy said. "A woman in distress—leastwise, I don't mean that. Look 'ere, miss, I knew you as a kiddie. I've 'ad you in me arms many a time. And it was me as found you in a burnin' 'ut, and me as 'ands you over to Mrs. Masters. An' a sweet pretty little thing you was. And she takes yer to 'er 'eart, and they brings you up as one of their family. For three years you lived with them out there. Many a time 'ave I come and watched you playin' together with the other children, afore you was all sent over to school. Ah, 'e was a good friend to you, Mr. Masters was ! Few men would 'ave done as much. You might 'ave been one of 'is own kids, for the way 'e behaved."

Gipsy pulled up suddenly, surprised and rendered a little uneasy by the change that had come over the girl's face. It was no longer cold and haughty, but the red lips were quivering and the dark eyes were swimming with unshed tears.

"There is something wrong here," the girl said unsteadily. "Mr. and Mrs. Masters were exceedingly good to me, but they were in no position to bring me up and pay my education. They always told me that my benefactor had placed me in their hands, with a sufficient sum of money to keep and educate me and equip me for my struggle with the world. To that unknown benefactor I owe everything. I was told that I was not to ask his name, and that he would make himself known to me in good time. And all that I have done in return for so much kindness was to send this photograph to Mr. Masters to forward to my best friend. Shortly before he died he wrote and told me he had done so. And, well, I don't think I need tell you any more. Is my benefactor dead, and did he ask you to bring that photograph back to me? What was he like? You must have known him well, or he would never have trusted you with my photograph. Describe him to me."

Gipsy drew a long, deep breath. The drama was proceeding apace, reeling off beautifully and in accordance with the best traditions. It was the great hour of Gipsy's life, the golden hour marred only by the reflection that it was played without an audience. If some of the gang down at the canteen could only see him now!

And yet there could be no curtain on the rigid lines laid down for the nice conduct of conventional melodrama. Gipsy was too fine an artist for that; his sense of the theatre amounted to genius. He could not take this fair creature in his arms and let her sob her gratitude out upon his homely shoulder. For here was a creature who, sooner or later, would take her pick of Britain's belted earls and hand down those glorious features to future generations.

"Well, I'll tell you, miss," Gipsy said. "Not as I'm goin' to mention no names. The chap as found you in a burnin' 'ut was no more than a common navvy. But he took a fancy to you, and as he 'ad saved a bit o' money, he asked 'is boss to 'elp 'im. And 'e did. And 'e didn't ask nothin' in return; you never saw a chap so surprised in 'is life as 'e was when Mr. Masters sent 'im this 'ere photograph. Whatever 'e'd done, that photograph paid 'im for. 'E told me that when 'e—'e lay dyin' with 'is 'and in mine."

"Are you quite sure he is dead?" the girl asked unsteadily.

"Dead as doornails," Gipsy said solemnly. "Dead as a cartload of 'em. Buried miles and miles away from 'ere at the bottom of a valley wot's now the centre of a lake. You couldn't get at 'im not if you'd got a million o' money. The last thing 'e told me, I was to find you out and give you back this photograph. 'E forgot to give me the address, but I knew I should find it somewhere. So if you'll take it, miss, and let me go while it's safe—"

One of the unshed tears dropped from one of the dark eyes and splashed on the face of the photograph.

"You may go, if you like," the girl said; "but I should prefer that you retained the photograph for the present. There are a great many questions I should like to ask you, but the servants may come in for the keys at any moment now, and your presence here might be misunderstood. After you have finished your work to-morrow, you will please come up here and ask for Miss Trevelyan. I want you to come and have tea with me, because I'm not at all satisfied that I have seen the last of my noble benefactor."

Gipsy stooped and lifted the slim fingers to his lips. He was anxious enough to get away now, and anxious to leave with a most efficient curtain falling on his exit. He knew that he had played his part properly—his correct instinct told him that.

He kissed the slim fingers, then he thrust the window-blind on one side and walked out into the night. In all his crowded life this was the greatest hour that his star had ever shone upon. It was the play that had occupied his waking dreams for many a year. For he, the hero, knew, and she, the heroine, knew, too, though no word of explanation had passed between them. And to go back on the morrow would be to spoil everything; it would be no more than a cheap and tawdry anti-climax, a lurid tag torn from a penny novelette. To be sure, Gipsy's mates down at the canteen would never know how fine a hero they had nourished in their breasts, but that was a small matter by comparison.

"It can't be done," Gipsy told himself, as he turned his face homewards. "Now, most people would go back and 'ave it out alone with a lot o' tears. Then they'd drop into the canteen and discuss it over a gallon or two of beer—and spoil everything. But that ain't the way of a man wot understands the real value of the drama. So I think I'll take that job wot's offered me out Cairo way."

So the girl waited in vain for the man, who trudged along the highways on the morrow with his face to the East.

DROPS OF WATER

In the course of Gipsy's researches in the fields of unwritten drama, he occasionally came across a character that he found it difficult to place, and the man called David Granadus was one of them. This was all the more annoying because outwardly, at any rate, Granadus was just the type to fill in a cast that lacked a suitable villain. Granadus was a huge man, with the muscles of an ox and a fine capacity for continuous labour, so long as it was plodding and mechanical, and not too feverishly strenuous. He was dark and swarthy as Gipsy himself, and undoubtedly there was some Zingari blood in his veins. He was quiet and moody, quick to resent anything in the way of a personality, and, when in drink, decidedly dangerous. Gipsy felt instinctively that great pluck was not one of the outstanding virtues of this man, big and powerful though he was. He had come to the Settlement a few weeks before, bringing with him his little girl, who appeared to be the one thing in life he cared for—that was, so long as he kept away from the canteen. When he did yield to temptation, then the child Zara was terribly neglected for days, and sometimes depended on charitable neighbours for food. More than one kind-hearted navvy's wife had suggested to Granadus that the child should board with her; but he refused to listen, and so father and daughter "kept" in the hut which had been assigned to the man, where they managed after a fashion of their own. A pretty child was Zara, a child of engaging manners and ways, wild as a hawk and without an atom of shyness. Further up the valley certain married engineers dwelt in what had once been farmhouses, and in some of these Zara was a welcome guest. More than one of these leaders of labour had spoken to Granadus on the subject of the child, only to be sullenly told to mind their own business.

Zara and Gipsy were great friends, and for the little girl's sake Gipsy tolerated Granadus. He was almost inclined to make the big, moody man into a suffering hero, whose one object in life was the little girl, the sole offspring of a broken romance. But this was only when Granadus chose to behave himself, and the villain theory found most favour, especially when the lure of the canteen was too strong for Granadus.

Just now Gipsy was particularly annoyed, because Zara had been ailing for some days, and Granadus was more than usually neglectful. He had been drinking heavily for the last week, he was insolent and insubordinate, so that one morning he found himself in contact with one of the divisional engineers, and chose to be flagrantly mutinous before a gang of men, most of whom had made trouble on more than one occasion. Engineer Leslie's firm-cut lips snapped together, and those grey eyes of his gleamed. He was not a big man, but every ounce of him was wire and whipcord, and he was an athlete to his finger-tips. And he knew how to use those hands of his, and here was an opportunity he had been seeking for a long time. There was no hatred in his heart, only a cool, grim determination to break this mutinous spirit and put Granadus in his place. Leslie knew all about Zara—indeed, the child was a free visitor at his own house, up in the spur of the big valley where one of the huge dams was under construction. And only that morning Mrs. Leslie had been telling her husband what a shame it was that that dear little girl should be so terribly neglected when she was obviously sickening for some illness, and, furthermore, she had suggested that her husband should speak firmly to Granadus about it. And now the light of battle was shining in Leslie's eyes.

"Do you want me to make you?" he asked crisply.

The other men, grinning over their work, listened hopefully. They grew more hopeful still as Granadus flung an insult over his shoulder at his chief and dropped his pick. A second later, and something struck Granadus under his left ear with the force of a kicking mule. The red light danced before his eyes as he advanced to battle, all his primitive passions were aroused now; his one simple desire was to kill Frank Leslie out of hand. He was big enough and strong enough to do it, but it was a question of brute strength clumsily applied against science and agility and grim, calculating coolness. Still, it was a good fight as long as it lasted, though from the very first the engineer had all the best of it. He waited patiently till his antagonist began to gasp and blow and stagger at the knees, and then he closed. It was as if a dozen iron blows were striking the unhappy Granadus simultaneously. He could feel them on his face, rattling on his ribs, then all the force was jolted out of his body by one tremendous blow on the point of the chin, and he lay there on the heather, spent and beat to the world.

"You asked for that," Leslie said quietly. "There are one or two more here who seem to be anxious for an argument. If they are ready—well, I am."

But apparently the argument was conclusive enough, and Leslie went his way with the pleasing assurance that he had not been wasting his time. All the same, he had made a bitter enemy, who would take his revenge all in good time, as Gipsy was not long in finding out. He went out of his way to warn the engineer, who was a favourite of his, but Leslie merely laughed. For the rest of the week Granadus brooded and drank deeply, and the sick child up in the hut yonder was more neglected than ever. Gipsy's imagination was touched now; he could scent tragedy in the air, he had a feeling that it was not far off. He reflected that Leslie's little thatched farmhouse was situated in a tiny amphitheatre in one of the spurs of the valley—in fact, the very spot that the spirit of tragedy might indicate as the scene of a cold-blooded murder. It was on the Saturday night that Gipsy heard something from the wife of one of the navvies that sent him uneasily scouting up the valley.

There had been a good deal of rain lately, and here and there were large volumes of flood-water behind such temporary stanks* as had been made to keep the spates back, so that the hands could work the valley cuttings under normal conditions. If one of these stanks gave way, then the consequences might be serious, especially in the case of a lonely house like that which had been given over to Leslie and his wife. If trouble came in the night, the spur would be washed out by the flood, and every living soul there beyond the reach of recovery. There was no real danger, for the work had been effectively done, and Gipsy was almost inclined to ask himself what he was afraid of.

[* stank: A dam or mound to stop water.]

He forged his way up the valley quietly and with that absence of noise which is an instinct of the born poacher. He came at length to the narrow track that led down the spur towards the house where Leslie and his wife were installed. So far everything seemed all right, and Gipsy smiled at his fears. But only for a moment, and then there broke on his quick ear the unmistakable sound of a pick striking on stones. The noise came again and again, many times repeated, before Gipsy could locate it. Those quick eyes of his were almost like those of a cat in the dark; he crouched and advanced on his hands and knees, and then it became plain as daylight.

There was Granadus at work on a huge boulder of rock which formed the foundation-stone of one of the stanks. Once that gave way a head of water three feet in diameter would spout with the force of a battering-ram through the opening; it would tear away the rest of the stank like so much rotten cheese. Five minutes more, and something like the full force of fifty million gallons of water would roar over the shoulder of the spur and carry everything before it like thistledown before a raging gale.

As Gipsy rose to his feet, he could see that the huge boulder was quivering and shaking, and that already a thin trickle of moisture ran over it like a perspiration. He could hear Granadus grunting with his exertions, he could see the pick swung over those massive shoulders for a final effort.

But that effort never came. Gipsy did not wait to count the heavy odds against him. He grabbed for a fragment of granite and brought it down with a cruel swing on to the head of Granadus. As the big man dropped, Gipsy turned him over and hammered on his face in a convulsion of rage and fury. When at length Granadus came to himself, Gipsy was sitting on his chest with his bands gripping the other's throat.

"Yer murderous devil!" he screamed. "So that's yer game, is it? I'll kill yer, yer dog ! Now listen to me. Get up I I'm not afraid of yer, and I'll know 'ow ter deal with yer presently. If that there stone gives way, then it's all up with the people down at the thatched cottage. Lor, talk about Nemesis! Now 'ere's a situation, if yer only knew it—an' yer don't—as 'ud make the fortune of any play. But I ain't goin' ter tell yer wot it is—least, not yet. I don't suppose yer never read a book by a chap wot's called Dickens. Never 'eard o' Ralph Nickleby, I expect. Well, yer will later on. It's lucky I come along ter save yer from a fate wot's worse than death. If yer've got a spark o' goodness in yer, yer '11 give a 'and. If yer won't, I'll blooming well make yer!"

But apparently there was no more fight left in Granadus. Beyoud doubt the wild fury of Gipsy's onslaught had sobered him.

He stood there uneasy and dejected, a beaten man, ready to do now exactly what he was told.

"Come on!" Gipsy cried. "It's all a matter o' minutes. If that there rock gives way, then nothin' can save them people down the spur yonder. And there's no time ter go down an' warn 'em, either. 'Ere, yer shove that light crane along them rails, whilst I goes an' gets 'old of a jack. Then we'll jack up one o' the wheels an' turn the 'ead o' the crane over agin that stone. See wot I mean? Upset the crane agin the stone an' form a sort of iron support for it. With a bit o' luck that stone'll 'old till I can get 'old of a cartridge or two an' blow a breach in the stank on the far side o' the slope. If I can manage that, then the situation's saved—if yer understand wot I mean, which yer don't. Now, then, get a move on, unless yer wants ter finish at the end of a rope!"

Granadus started to work mechanically; he slaved like a man in a dream. All his moodiness seemed to have gone now; he listened to Gipsy and followed his instructions as if he had been a gigantic child. It required all his abnormal strength to turn the crane, but the wheels began to move at last, and presently the huge mass of steel came to a halt in front of the trembling rock that was now holding the great flood of water back by so slender a tenure. Gipsy came staggering out of the darkness, dragging a jack behind him. The little man was sweating from head to foot with the force of his exertions; he trembled lest he should be too late. For if once the barrier of rock gave way, then the passage of a minute would see a roaring torrent of water sweeping headlong down the spur. Even now the rock groaned and creaked. Through a dozen orifices many yellow spurts gushed out. Then Gipsy worked the jack under the wheels of the crane, and cursed Granadus for standing there doing nothing.

"Give a 'and, yer owl!" he panted. "That's better! Now, then, up she goes, an' over she goes! Got it!"

The towering weight of metal heaved over, paused a second, and then, with a crashing force, dropped right in the centre of the rock. The wheels locked in the mud, and, so far as Gipsy could see, the situation was saved. That steel barrier would hold, perhaps, till the damage that Granadus had done had been properly repaired, and the only danger that Gipsy could see now lay in the chance of the rock slipping sideways, in which case the remedy would be no better than the disease.

It was all a question of time now. It would take a good quarter of an hour to get to the bottom of the spur and arouse the people in the thatched cottage. It would take a little longer to wake them and bring them back, and Gipsy was calculating in his quick way whether it would not be far wiser to break into one of the huts further up the valley and lay hands on a dynamite cartridge or a gun-cotton charge with a short time-fuse attached. If he could do this within the next ten minutes, then all would be well, for it would not be a difficult matter to blow out a hole in the far side of the stank and empty that cruel flood of water like a bucket into the valley, where it would run back in the main stream and do no particular harm.

Ten to twelve breathless, precious minutes could be saved this way, and that was the plan that Gipsy decided to adopt.

"Now, yer stop 'ere an' fight," he said. "Pile up as many o' them stones as yer can. Every little 'elps. I'll be off for the dynamite. If yer can 'old on 'ere till my popgun goes off, then yer neck's all right. If yer can't—"

With this significant suggestion, Gipsy raced away up the valley as if the whole weight of the world was on his shoulders. By the time he reached the first hut and had smashed in the lock with a big stone, he was trembling from head to foot and gasping painfully for breath that seemed to be denied him. For the moment he had forgotten that he was playing the part of hero in his own drama, but that knowledge would come presently. Just now he was a hard-pressed little navvy working like a Trojan to save five innocent lives. He found what he wanted presently—a powerful hand-charge of some high explosive with a short time-fuse. There would be trouble to-morrow over this breaking into one of the ammunition huts, but Gipsy trusted to his native wit and plausibility of explanation to get himself out of the mess. As he raced across the embankment to the far side of the flood, he was suddenly conscious of the heat of the night and his own dripping, perspiring body. He was himself again now; he was once more the born playwright working out his plot. He found the very spot he wanted presently—a deep hole in the side of the embankment—and far into this he thrust the explosive. He was not afraid of any noise, for the bank was too soft for that. There would be no more than a dull thud, and then the bank would crumble away like butter in the sun. Gipsy felt the earth quiver, then part of the bank slid greasily down into the valley, and a yellow, turgid flow of water followed. The thing was done and the situation saved, if only the steel battering-ram had stood on the far side of the stank.

Gipsy ran round to see how Granadus was getting on. The big man was spent and exhausted, but the barrier still held and the great rock was beginning to dry. Gipsy dropped down into the heather and wiped the moisture from his steaming face.

"Well, that's all right," he gasped. "Now I 'ope as you're properly ashamed of yerself . My lad, d'yer realise as I've saved yer from standin' in the dock on a charge o' murder?"

Granadus looked up vaguely. He might have been a man just coming to the surface after being submerged in a flood of evil dreams. The horror of the nightmare was still in his eyes, and he rubbed them as if to wipe out some ghastly sight.

"I was mad!" he snid hoarsely. "It's the drink as does it, Gipsy. I oughtn't to ever touch a drop—a doctor friend o' mine told me so long ago. But I've 'ad a lot o' bitter trouble in my time, an' there's moments when I sort o' fly to it. And then I ain't safe—I ought to be locked up. An' It ain't as if I bore any grudge against Leslie."

"Oh, yer don't, don't yer?" Gipsy jeered.

"I can't think 'ow I come to do it," Granadus repeated. "Now, look 'ere, mate, if you won't say nothin' abaht this, then I swear as I'll never touch another drop. I don't want those chaps down there in the canteen—"

Gipsy gave a snort of contempt. He demanded to know what Granadus took him for. For the drama was at full blast now, and the little man had his limitations. It was more than flesh and blood could stand to forego a dramatic triumph like this and none be any tbe wiser. And Gipsy was beginning to see his way. He turned solemnly to his companion.

"I don't want to be 'ard," he said magnanimously, "an' I never 'it a bloke when 'e's down; but yer've got ter come along o' me, all the same. This way, if yer please."

"Wot—down to the engineer's?" Granadus asked.

"Yer've guessed it the first time," Gipsy said. "It ain't late, so we'll just take a little stroll along the spur an' 'ave a few words along o' Mr. Leslie. You're goin' ter tell 'im as you're sorry yer give 'im that bit o' lip the other day, an' say as in future yer've swore off. Got that?"

Granadus shrugged his big shoulders, but made no further objection. He strode silently down the spur by the side of Gipsy, until they reached the low thatched house where Leslie and his wife dwelt. It was a bungalow with a long verandah in front, the type of farmer's house which at one time they built there up in the hills. Very soon the whole thing would be submerged, but it looked snug and homelike now, with the lamps burning in the windows, one of which was open, disclosing the bedroom beyond. Gipsy stepped quietly on to the verandah and looked in. Then he suddenly seemed to stiffen with rapt attention, and, when he came back to Granadus, his features were twitching strangely.

"In all my life," he whispered, "I never see the like o' this! I said somethin' ter yer just now 'bout Nemesis. Lor, I didn't 'arf know the meaning o' the word! Now look 'ere. 'Ow long ago yer been on the drink? 'Ow long is it since yer've been inside that 'ut o' yourn?"

"Three days," Granadus said shame-facedly.

"Ah, I thought so. Now yer come this way an' tread soft. Don't say nuthin', but take yer tip from me. If yer opens yer mouth, then yer spoils the finest situation I ever see."

Granadus obeyed meekly enough. Standing there in the darkness on the verandah, he could see into the lighted bedroom through the open window. On the bed lay a child, a pretty dark child with long hair flowing over her white night-dress. She was half supported in the arms of a smiling woman in evening-dress, who was holding a glass of milk to her lips. On the foot of the bed Leslie was seated, watching the picture with a pleasant smile upon his face.

"And now you are going off to sleep, little one," he said. "Oh, you need not worry about your daddy—he's all right. He shall come up and see you to-morrow, and you can tell him all about it. We shan't want the doctor any more—in fact, you are going to be quite well in a day or two."

The child reached up and kissed the woman's smiling face, then she lay down contentedly and closed her eyes. A minute or two later and she was fast asleep.

"I think she'll do now," Leslie murmured. "She's had a sharp turn—as near pneumonia as makes no matter—and she owes her lucky escape to you, old girl."

"Oh, I couldn't do anything less, Frank," Mrs. Leslie said. "Those women were doing their best, of course, but they have their own children to look after. If I had my way with that man Granadus, I'd send him to gaol. Is he in his right senses, do you think? I can't understand a parent like that. I'm told he fairly idolises the child one week, and utterly neglects her the next. It really is disgraceful, Frank. It ought not to be allowed. Can't you speak to the man? Can't you get him to come up here and make him see how wicked he is behaving?"

"Well, I had some idea of the sort," Leslie said. "But Granadus is a queer chap. I don't think he is very vindictive when he is sober, but there are certain men who ought never to touch alcohol, and he's one of them. When he is drunk, he's a dangerous man. I have given him one lesson, but I don't think he's much the better for it. If we can only touch the brute, if we can only penetrate that thick hide of his, then the kiddy ought to be safe for the future."

"Perhaps if he knew what we had done for Zara "

"Um, perhaps!" Leslie interrupted. "You have certainly saved her life. But a man like Granadus is just as likely to think that we have done all this because we are afraid of him. Still, I will see him to-morrow."

Gipsy laid a quick, detaining hand upon Granadus's arm. He fairly dragged the big man off the balcony into the heather. He could see how the other's face was quivering.

"No, yer don't!" he said fiercely. "Not to-night, anyhow. Yer don't spoil the finest situation I ever come across with any of yer blunderings, so I tell yer. Yer can come up in the mornin' an' do an' say just as you've a mind. But not to-night, mate. To-night you've got ter leave those two grand characters alone. Yer've got ter go back to yer 'ut an' thank 'Eaven on yer knees for keepin' yer from murder—from takin' the lives, not only of yer best friends, but of yer own child, too. An' I suppose yer don't believe as they're afraid of yer, do yer?"

"Don't rub it in too 'ard, Gipsy," Granadus said humbly. "An' if you won't say no thin' down at the canteen "

"Me!" Gipsy said scornfully. "Just as if—But wot do you know about the feelings of a dramatist?"

THE UNPREMEDITATED CURTAIN

This is one of the stories of the little man with the dark curls and the gold ear-rings, a story of Gipsy and what he always considered to be the greatest dramatic triumph of his life. For it will be remembered that the man in question was a born playwright, and shared Shakespeare's opinion as to all the world's a stage and all the men and women merely players. It was only certain defects in Gipsy's education— But this I have mentioned before. It all came about so simply, too.

It was at the time when Gipsy, together with some ten thousand other excavators, was working on the Welsh watershed which was to supply a great Northern town in course of time. And here was scope for all the Zingari's peculiar talents and natural instincts in the way of fieldcraft, which a crass bench of local magistrates would insist upon calling poaching. For there were covers on the hillside—to say nothing of grouse in the heather—the little streams were full of trout, and up at the head of the main tributary the lordly salmon lay. All of which, in its season, was a lasting joy to Gipsy, to whom the fine art of the primeval man was an open book. He was a good sportsman, too—killed for the pot and the joy of the game, and eke for the benefit of his neighbours. And so far no keeper had laid violent hands upon him, which was Gipsy's one fear. It was the spice of terror that gave zest to the feast, the one haunting trouble that kept him bright and clear.

Now, it was beautiful March weather, with the streams running as fine as a star, and the moon was at the full. And, moreover, in the hut that Gipsy shared with a married navvy was a small girl, to whom the little man was sincerely attached. The small girl was just getting over a severe attack of influenza, her appetite was capricious, and, moreover, the doctor had said something about a fish diet. This was not so simple as it seemed, until Gipsy bent his masterly mind to grapple with the situation. Up yonder in the headwaters were salmon, and down there was Gipsy. There is no reason to labour the analogy.

An afternoon or two later Gipsy set out on a five-mile walk to Prestyn, and there in a fishmonger's shop he found the very thing he wanted. They were small objects, tiny crustaceans, half a dozen of which Gipsy purchased at the outlay of a shilling. With these in his pocket he repaired back to the camp, and at nine o'clock the same night he was picking his way daintily along the banks of the headwater with an eighteen-feet salmon-rod in his hand. The salmon-rod was a secret so far as the camp was concerned, and its hiding-place was a hollow alder tree on the side of the stream. Altogether, it was a pretty adventure as it stood. The smell of spring was in the air, and the scent of the good red earth was fragrant in the little man's nostrils. For Nature was talking to him as he went along; there was not a blade of grass or a twig full of sap without its message. And, moreover, Gipsy was a master of his craft; the tapering line he threw dropped in the stream as clean and sweet as a razor edge, the bait fell without a sound. It was Gipsy's wits against the big fish fresh-run from the sea, and the odds were in favour of those elusive shadows, for the water was low and fine, and no "Doctor" or "Jock Scott" so much as excited the flutter of a fin. In the ordinary way Gispy would have scorned to do what he was doing now, but he wanted the fish badly, and he had to jockey the odds so as to place the match on a more level footing. It was his wit against that of the salmon, and Gipsy was going to win.

He had not walked a quarter of a mile, or made more than a score of casts, before he was into a fish. He could see the heavy swirl and the little ripples as the bait was sucked down, and then the fight began. It was a pretty little scrap, and it was going hard with the furiously fighting fish, when a hand was laid on Gipsy's shoulder. He dropped his point suddenly, the salmon gave a sudden lunge, and twenty feet of line came back like a boomerang into the sportsman's face. He was annoyed and angry at this unseemly interruption, and then it was borne in upon him that more important considerations were at stake. Without waiting for a word of explanation, Gipsy dropped his rod and turned on the keeper. The latter was full of fight—he had the weight of law and authority on his side, and his pluck was beyond doubt— but he was up against a wily foe, who had learnt his cunning of fence in a dozen countries. There was a touch of jiu-jitsu, with just a suspicion of savate and perhaps a suggestion of Cumberland. Anyway, a few minutes later and the keeper was lying with head buried in the sprouting heather, and Gipsy was kneeling on the small of his back. The one idea uppermost in the little man's mind had been to conceal his face from the foe, and so far he felt tolerably sure that he had been successful. He did not want to be identified, which in his case would be nearly as bad as being led ignominiously to the police station at the foot of the big dam.

"You can get up," he gasped. "And don't you look over your shoulder, mate. If you do, I'll push your face through the back of your head! What do you mean by comin' and interruptin' a gentleman in the middle of his sport? Now, you see that hut yonder? Will you just walk straight to that? And mind what I tell you. Remember Lot's wife, cully."

This timely allusion was evidently not wasted, for the keeper strode doggedly on in the direction of the hut, whilst Gipsy followed behind, his nimble mind busy with the immediate future. Here in effect was a scene from a potential drama, and Gipsy was treating it accordingly. The situation was clear in his mind now; he knew exactly what to do. Moreover, he had, in his capacity as foreman, the master-key to the store huts in his pocket. Presently he passed the key over the shoulder of his prisoner and signified the sullen captive to open the door.

"Got any matches?" he demanded.

The prisoner gave a short negative, and Gipsy chuckled. Inside the hut the light was dim, but not dim enough to obscure the outline of some scores of huge cartridge cases piled up on the floor. They were empty of dynamite for the moment, but the prisoner was not likely to know that. From a box Gipsy took a double handful of small detonators and scattered them liberally all over the floor.

"Now, you sit on that box," he said. "I don't mind telling you that those drainpipe-looking concerns are dynamite cartridges. There is enough dynamite here to blow up half the county. These little jokers I've scattered all over the floor is what's called detonators. Step on one of them and you are done for, old pard. Understand that? So long as you squats there you are safe. Somebody's sure to come along about six in the morning, and then it will be all right. You ain't got no matches, and, when I lock that door, this place will be as dark as that empty mind of yourn. So long!"

With that, Gipsy locked the door of the hut with an easy mind and a pleased feeling that few professional playwrights could have done any better. Then he went back to his fishing, secure in the knowledge that he was safe, and that his practical philanthropy had the approval of the gods. He repaired his line and baited a wicked-looking triangle, and at his fourth cast was into another splendid fish.

He could concentrate all his energy upon the sport now, and half an hour later a quivering bar of silver lay on the grass in the moonhght. And then came another interruption, slightly more unpleasant than the last.

"Well, of all the infernal cool cheek!" a voice said.

Gipsy looked up suddenly. He was face to face with an exceedingly useful-looking individual, brown and lean and hard, and evidently in the pink of condition. This was a very different proposition to the somewhat corpulent keeper, and, like the good general that he was, Gipsy recognised it at a glance. He made a dive through the legs of the fresh foeman, bringing him heavily to the ground, then struck out at top speed along the bank of the river. But there was no shaking off the lean man, and though Gipsy turned about like a hare, the other held on doggedly behind, till the little man's lungs began to contract and his heart was pounding against his ribs painfully. Then the man behind dropped his left shoulder and dived for Gripsy's legs in the manner of a star three-quarter back—as indeed, he had been—and brought Gipsy to the ground without a breath in his body. The stars were reeling overhead and the pines on the hillside seemed to be tossing in a fantastic saraband.

"Now, then," the lean man said, "you sit quietly down there and listen to me. I want you to know that this for the time being is my stretch of water. Not to be unduly ostentatious, I beg to say that I paid two hundred pounds for it. Incidentally, I might mention that I have been flogging this blessed stream for six weeks now, without so much as seeing a fin. Relaxation, of course, and a change from the nerve-strain of writing melodrama, but at the same time it leaves one just a little unsatisfied. And here you come along, a mere poaching navvy, who has probably never heard of the divine bard of Avon, catching fish as if you had been used to it all your life—in the moonlight, too! Now, what the deuce do you mean by it? Or, rather, I should say, how on earth do you manage it?"

Gipsy sat up and grinned. He no longer saw grim visions of six weeks in Prestyn Gaol; he was only cognisant of the fact that he was face to face with a brother-humorist, and he had heard it once said in a theatre that one touch of Nature makes the whole world kin. And here he was for the first time in his life actually in the presence of a living, breathing dramatist. He forgot the salmon for the moment.

"You are a bit of all right, guv'nor, you are," he said admiringly. "Fairly wore me down, you did. I knew it was all up directly I caught sight of that brown mug o' yourn. Lor bless you, sir, I'd know a real sportsman if I met him in a dark cellar on a winter's night! You might call me a poacher—perhaps I am, but not one of them sneakin', perishin' blighters as makes money at the game. I'm a gipsy, I am. Born in a tent and lived in the open air all my life. There ain't a bird as flies or a fish as swims as can get the best of me, if I brings my mind to it. And I weren't exactly poaching to-night, guv'nor. You see, there's a kid belonging to my landlady wot's been ill, and she can't do with no regular food. So, thinks I, wot's the matter with a bit o' salmon? And there you are, guv'nor."

The brown-faced man laughed, and Gipsy laughed too, for he was feeling tolerably easy in his mind. It was quite evident that he had made an impression on the other fellow, who appeared to believe every word of this explanation. And in any case Gipsy had no intention of neglecting this God-sent opportunity. He was in the presence of a dramatist, a man who wrote real plays that were produced at real theatres. He was not Gipsy's conception of the traditional playwright, who, from the little man's point of view, should be pale and bent and long of hair, with dreamy eyes half concealed by spectacles.

"Do you know, that's jolly interesting," the dramatist said. "You have given me an idea for a rattling good situation. You see, I came down here to fish—knowing nothing whatever about that sort of thing—and work on a play at the same time. The idea was to toil morning and evening at the desk, and in the afternoon go out and catch huge fishes, which I intended to send to my friends with my kindest regards. In this respect the programme has broken down rather badly, Mr. Navvy. My collaborator and myself have got this thing on our minds. We need encouraging, we need something— Oh, well, you see, we are writing the big autumn drama for Chancery Lane."

Gipsy fairly gasped, for this was beyond his wildest dream. Drama was his theatrical pabulum; from his point of view, the great Chancery Lane autumn drama was the finest production in the world. He had contrived to see most of them, he knew the majority of the striking situations by heart. The two mighty geniuses responsible for this gigantic annual effort were the dim and distant gods of Gipsy's idolatry. And here he was actually face to face with either the famous Mr. Goodheart or the equally famous Mr. Rankin—it did not matter which. The mere fact that nobody would believe Gipsy, when he came to tell the story afterwards, did nothing to poison the crystal stream of his bliss.

"There's plenty of fish in the river, sir," he said.

"Really?" the dramatist replied sadly. "So the keeper says. But I began to believe that someone has been taking advantage of our youth and innocence. I've tried the fish with flies and I've tried them with worms, and to-morrow I was going to tempt them with a novel nutriment of bread and treacle. I'll tell jou what I'll do with you, my friend. If you will show me how to catch fish,I'll give you a ten-pound note, and you can come here and angle whenever you like. What's that? Oh, I don't care. Call me a poacher, if you like—anything is good enough for me, from Christian Science to a nice, big, comfortable net. I want to go back to the club and swagger; I want to talk about my river, don't you know, and that day that Mr. Rankin and myself killed sixteen clean-run fish. Show me how I can stroll out in the moonlight and pick up a brace of those beauties between the whiff of a cigarette. Apparently it can be done."

"That's right, sir," Gipsy grinned; "but I don't mind telling yer straight that I'm poachin'. Lor bless yer 'eart, yer can't catch salmon by moonlight with a fly, and I'll lay any money as your agreement with 'is lordship bars you from taking 'em with a prawn, and that's what I'm using. There ain't no bait in the wide world for a fresh-run fish like a prawn. The fish thinks he's back in the sea again. Now, look 'ere, sir. I've got four prawns in my pocket, and, wot's more, I've got that keeper o' yourn safe locked up in a hut yonder. It ain't a bad story, sir, and perhaps you'd like to 'ear it."

The great dramatist sat smoking his cigarette and laughing like a boy till Gipsy had finished.

"Oh, this is a night to remember!" he cried. "Look here, you've got the making of a dramatist in you. It's not a bad situation, either. I'll make it all right with the keeper presently. Meanwhile, I'm out for blood. Attach the fascinating prawn to the deadly instrument, and let's see what I can make of it. Show me how to catch fish, and if the gratitude of a lifetime—In short, let's get to work."

An hour later and three noble bars of silver, tinged with steely-blue, lay at the feet of the delighted dramatist. He fairly danced round them. Visions of happy afternoons, with the keeper dispatched on long expeditions, danced delightedly before his eyes. There was only one thing for it— Gipsy must come up to the farm cottage, where the great drama was being written, and drink to the great adventure. Nothing loath, Gipsy followed. Here was something to talk about. Here was a proud boast to make, though in all probability no one would believe him. He had made a friend in that walk of life to which occasionally he had turned longing eyes, and, moreover, he had the right to fish those splendid waters when and where he chose, and, more than this, he had been recognised as a fellow-dramatist in the bud.

They came presently to the cottage, the door of which was open, and inside someone appeared to be moaning as if in pain.

"That's Rankin," Goodheart said cheerfully. "He always carries on like that when he is stumped for an idea. As I told you before, we came down here to work out our autumn drama. We've got two big situations, but we want a third to lead up to a huge curtain in front of the fourth act. That's Rankin's job, and he's feeling very badly about it. He ought to have hit on something now long before this, as I told him to-night. But come in, Gipsy. The sight of you may do him good."

The big, stone-flagged sitting-room was ablaze with lamps, and at the table, strewn with papers, a little man, with a large head and a long, drooping moustache, sat groaning dismally. He was biting the stem of a pipe between his teeth, and his aspect was one of genial ferocity.

"I was coming out to look for you," he said. "It's no good, old chap—I can't think of anything. All my ideas are so beastly stagy. What I want is some natural son-of-the-soil sort of chap to form a connecting link. But what, in the name of fortune, have you got there? You don't mean to say—"

"Caught 'em all myself," Goodheart said proudly. "Our friend here put me up to the game. As a piscatorial fascinator, my little gipsy is a genius. It's as easy as possible when you only know how. The 'Open, Sesame' to the heart of a salmon is prawns, and don't you forget it, only it's a dead secret, my boy, so not a word to a soul. But if your stomach is not too proud and your conscience sufficiently elastic, then—prawns!"

Gipsy stood there grinning in the background. He was invited to tell his story again. He was delighted to find in the melancholy man so much capacity for innocent mirth.

"You are a man after my own heart, Mr. Gipsy," he said. "I also am fired with a desire to inundate my friends with salmon. Perhaps, if I caught a fish or two, it would enable me to throw off this profound melancholy, which is not my habitual aspect. Can't you give us an idea—thundering big idea—something between an earthquake and an unexpected general election? You have got the dramatic instinct, if ever I saw it in a man. Unlock your secret bosom and speak, Sphinx."

All this was in the spirit of chaff and uttered with a melancholy cadence that did not deceive Gipsy for a moment. He had had a great evening, he had found himself on terms of almost equality with these Olympians, and, moreover, he was well into his second glass of whisky and soda. And these gods had stooped from the heights of Parnassus to actually invite him to take a hand in the great literary event of the year!

"Well, gentlemen," he said, "you've been real sportsmen to me, and I'm always ready to do my best to oblige. I am downright fond of the theatre, I am, and whenever my work takes me into a town, I always treats myself regular to a bob's worth o' gallery. Not as I cares much for comedy or them shows, which is all music and girls "

"Bit of a misogynist," Rankin suggested.

"That's it," Gipsy grinned. "It sounds a good word, sir, though it never come my way before. But, as I was saying, it's drama as gets my money every time—'Lights of London,' 'The Silver King,' and all that sort. If I were a scholar, which I ain't by a long chalk, I'd 'ave 'ad a shot at it myself. And for a real big thing—why, you've got it out of doors!"

"What do you mean by that?" Goodheart asked.

"The whole bloomin' camp," Gipsy went on. "Here's ten thousand of us, to say nothin' of women an' children, an' we're spendin' a matter o' six million o' money to make these 'ere waterworks. When the great dam's finished, there'll be half a dozen lakes along the top end of the valley, if you understand what I mean, gents. Talk about 'uman passions—why, the 'ole camp's full of them! 'Ere you've got a scene as, to my mind, 'ud take a lot o' beating. Let's suppose for a moment as that keeper chap wot's waitin' so patiently out yonder 'as been made a prisoner there by the villain of the piece. Let's suppose as those detonators is real an' them cartridges is live dynamite. He steps on one of 'em an' fires the dynamite, which blows up the big dam an' releases the lakes. Now, that's wot I call a good scene, if you'll allow me to say so. The villain o' the piece, 'e 'as powerful reasons for destroyin' the dam, and the 'ero 'e wants to save it. Lor bless yer, I've worked out that 'ere thing over and over again in a dozen ways, an' I don't know which is the best. I can see the dam blown up an' the waters comin' down, an' the 'ero an' the 'eroine up there on the top, savin' the situation, if that's the right name for it. I may be wrong, but if there isn't a good curtain in that, then I'm blowed, an' that's the end of it!"

Rankin's face was illuminated with a holy joy. He reached out and grasped Gipsy warmly by the hand.

"The unpremeditated curtain!" he cried. "Always the best, because spontaneous. The problem is solved. Yet what a pity to see so much brilliant genius wasted—I mean you, Mr. Gipsy!"

MERE DETAILS

When Reuben Tomfit drifted casually into the great colony up there at the head of the watershed behind Prestyn, in search of work, Gipsy rose to him at once and attached him to his own gang of navvies. The little man with the ear-rings, with that fine eye of his for dramatic possibilities, could see in his new hand a human document of the most fascinating kind. Beyond all question there was a story lurking behind the man with the ridiculous name, and all Gipsy's instincts were aroused. He could see in Tomfit not merely a muscular Christian, with a fine capacity for sound, honest work, but also one who is unmistakably a gentleman with a history. Like all his class, Gipsy had an unerring eye for what he called a "toff," and beyond question Tomfit was one of these. Not even his shaggy suit and the absence of a collar could disguise the fact, and it was plain from the way he carried himself that he had done nothing to be ashamed of. He was a young man with a clear-cut, weary face, a clean blue eye, and as fine a set of muscles as Gipsy had ever seen. He spoke, too, in a lazy, languid way, and his capacity for taking chaff touched on the fringe of genius. He could fight, too, as Gipsy had seen on more than one occasion, and after that the Settlement began to take him for granted.

But not so Gipsy. His literary curiosity impelled him to lay hands upon the sealed book. For here was the hero of one of Gipsy's most sentimental dramas. Here was the unhappy victim of cross-eyed fortune, driven from his ancestral home to fight the battle of life and hack his way back to prosperity. If the Settlement had been a gold mine instead of the centre of a gigantic water system, then Gipsy would have seen his way more clearly. As it was, the little man could not make up his mind how to tap the golden stream and lead his hero back to happiness and the arms of the inevitable beautiful heroine who was doubtless lingering somewhere there in the misty and illusive background.

Gipsy's efforts, however, were not wasted, for something like a friendship sprang up between the two men, and the native dramatist was proud of it. He inveigled Tomfit into one or two of his poaching excursions, and actually learned something new in the way of "dapping" for trout from his mysterious friend. It was quite plain that Tomfit was a fine all-round sportsman, and Gipsy respected him accordingly. He was proud to be seen about with this man, and flattered by the curiosity of his mates, who, naturally enough, wanted to know something of the antecedents of the new-comer. The temptation was too great to be resisted, and there came a time one evening, in the canteen, when the floodgates of Gipsy's eloquence fell, and he spoke. The fact that Tomfit never came near the canteen was all in the romancer's favour.

"O' course, it's all in confidence between me an' you, blokes," Gipsy said. "But I don't mind tellin' yer as the cove wot calls 'isself Tomfit, and comes 'ere earnin' 'is bread by the sweat o' that marble brow of 'is is Lord Algy Fitzlangham. 'E is called that because, yer see, 'e 'appens to be the second son of a certain earl whose name I ain't at liberty to mention."

Somebody in the background laughed, and a snigger went round the little circle of smokers. It was felt that Gipsy was in his very best form to-night. He smiled loftily.

"O' course," he said, " if yer thinks I'm a bloomin' liar, then, there ain't no more to be said."

"Go on, Gipsy," the chorus said soothingly.

"Right O," Gipsy resumed. "Seein' that I 'ad it from the bloke's own lips, I don't care whether yer believe me or not. Perhaps yer will say presently as 'e ain't a toff."

"Any fool could see that," a listener muttered.

"Very well, then. Anybody else got anything to say? Anybody anxious to collect a thick ear? No? Well, it's like this. The earl wot I was talkin' about, 'e's got two sons. 'E's a old cove, with one foot in the grave. 'E and 'is ancestors afore 'im, they've lived in the old castle for about a thousand years. They was rich at one time, but for a long time they've been so poor that they're 'ard put to it sometimes to keep them retainers of theirs in food. Pretty near 'ad to sell all the family plate wot they've been feeding off for generations. An' the estates are all mortgaged to a chap in London wot's a miser—you know the sort o' cully I mean."

"Like a chap in a play I once saw," someone interrupted. "Jew, 'e was—name o' Fagin, I think."

"It's a pleasure to 'ave a listener like you, Ginger," Gipsy said. "Well, this money-lending cove, 'e's got 'is 'ooks on the family estates, and 'is lordship 'e don't know wot to do. Then from Australia comes a niece, one o' them tall, dark, handsome gels with 'air like the raven's wing, an' she ups and tells the old man as she's the daughter of a brother of 'is wot went out yonder years ago, in consequence of some little unpleasantness with the police, and that now 'e's dead, and she's worth 'bout two millions o' money."

"An' the old lord 'e collars 'er for 'is daughter," Ginger suggested, stimulated by Gipsy's praise.

"You've got an intelligent grip, Ginger," Gipsy said patronisingly, "but you ain't quite right. You ain't quite enough up in the ways o' the aristocracy. Yer see, it was the eldest son as the old geeser wanted the girl for. You see, as 'e was heir to the estates, 'e 'ad to marry money. It didn't matter nothing 'bout the second son—by which I mean my pal, o' course—because 'e could go off cattle-sticking or pig-shooting, same as younger sons always does in the plays. So it all looked very gay, an' as if the money-lending bloke in London 'ud be done out o' the estates, after all. But it seems as the gel Ermyntrood didn't cotton to the eldest son at all. You see, 'e was a bit of a mug in 'is way, short-sighted and wore glasses, and never couldn't eat anything without dinner pills. Sort of bloke as couldn't fish or shoot, and wanted to go into Parliament—well, 'e weren't no good. O' course, this 'ere Ermyntrood she wasn't going to look at a cove like that when there was a real flyer like Lord Algernon sittin' up an' takin' notice. So these two they gits off shootin' an' fishin' together, and, before they knows where they were, they was over 'ead and ears in love with one another, an' the eldest son—why, he weren't even in the bettin'! There weren't a footman on the premises who'd 'ave backed 'im for 'arf-a-crown!"

Gipsy paused to inhale his tobacco. He had his audience in the hollow of his hand now, and their rapt silence was soothing.

"Well, the old josser 'e finds out all about it, o' course, and a nice old temper 'e was in, too. So 'e takes Lord Algy on one side after dinner, when they was a-drinkin' o' their beer, same as you chaps an' me might be doin' 'ere, an' 'e speaks 'is mind free. 'E says if Lord Algernon don't 'op it, then all the props is knocked away an' the cuttin's full o' water. If Ermyntrood don't marry the eldest son, then the family estates are up the spout, an' no mistake. 'E rings the bell for another bottle o' beer, an' works on the young man's pride. O' course, 'e sees the force o' the argument, and, for the sake of 'is ancestors, makes up 'is mind to do a guy and leave Ermyntrood to think as 'e'd only been 'avin a bit o' fun with 'er all the time. If 'e does this, o' course she'll marry the eldest son, an'—well, there you are. And that's just wot 'e up and done."

"Some fools never know their luck," Ginger observed.

"Can't yer see as it was a sacrifice?" Gipsy asked him indignantly. "Can't yer see this is the way that proper toffs always behaves? You'd 'ave drunk the old man's beer an' told 'im to go and put 'is 'ead in a bag, you would!"

"That's right, mate," Ginger said promptly.

Gipsy was properly indignant. He had a good many sarcastic things to say touching the benighted ignorance of the class of man who knows nothing of the traditions and axioms of the British aristocracy as portrayed in the society novel. He was wrapped up in his subject, and unfolded his tale as if it had come hot from the lips of the unhappy Lord Algernon, and was being translated by a dramatist bubbling over with sympathy.

"'E's no mug," Gipsy conclu-ded. "He's a 'ero an' a martyr, an' I'm proud o' the fact as 'e 'as taken me into 'is confidence. An' as to 'is pluck—why, there's more'n one 'ere in the canteen wot's felt it!"

There was no gainsaying this, and further criticism of the mysterious Lord Algernon was suspended. It was a day or two later that the pluck in question was put to another test. Shortly before the dinner-hour was finished, and the whistles began to hoot hoarsely up and down the green slopes of the valley, a whisper ran from lip to lip, and the gangs of men came to their feet as if some hidden force was dragging at them.

In that zone of danger, embracing over ten thousand able-bodied men engaged in the titanic struggle against the forces of Nature, there were always perils, and one of them had dropped like a bolt from the blue now. Further up the valley was a long adit cut into the hillside, and intended later on to carry off a big volume of superfluous water in times of flood. A powerful stream across the adit, some fifty yards from the mouth, had given way before an unexpected landslide. In other words, at the top of the adit over thirty men had been cut off by that fall of earth, and the only way to reach them lay along a huge drain, which was now full of water. To dig down to those men meant the best part of a week's work, with every resource the engineers could employ. There was one forlorn hope, and that was to find someone strong enough and expert enough to dive along that black yawning drain and reach the prisoners the other end. Whoever undertook that ghastly peril, and succeeded, could convey enough dynamite about his person to blow out the end of the adit and thus free a body of men who otherwise would be doomed to a painful and lingering death.

The chance was a desperate and slender one, for the odds were long against any swimmer diving so far along that forbidding drain. There were scores of men—hundreds of them—there who would have faced an open peril without a moment's hesitation. But, for the most part, they hung back now, until the man called Tomfit pushed his way forward and surveyed that dark mouth critically as he finished his cigarette.

"I'll have a shot," he drawled. "Put up the stuff for me in a water-tight box, so that I can carry it round my neck. Get a move on, some of you! The more I look at it, the less I like it. Now, don't be all day!"

Quite leisurely he stripped himself, with the exception of his underclothing, and stood there waiting for the charge to be made ready. A moment later, and another semi-nude figure stood by his side. Gipsy grinned amiably.

"Two 'eads is better than one, mate," he said. "You go first, and I'll foller. Get going."

Tomfit waited for no more. He bent himself back like a strong, white bow, then plunged headlong into the inky water. He was followed a moment later by Gipsy, and then began a battle of pluck and sinew, of agony and endurance, on the one side, and the sullen force of Nature on the other. It was only a matter, perhaps, of a minute and a half, as time went, but to those two white heroes forcing their way in the pitch darkness it seemed more like hours. They did not know—they could not tell—what distance they had to go except by guess. Gipsy's head was reeling, his lungs were strained to the bursting-point; but still he struggled on and on, occasionally touching the heels of the man before him. Then Tomfit went down, and, with an inward snarl, Gipsy grabbed for him and turned over on his back, dragging a dead weight that seemed to be the last word of a tragedy. And then Gipsy realised that his head was out of that murderous flood, and the breath of life streaming through his quivering nostrils. It was a fine thing finely done, and the little man was feeling giddy at the contemplation of it. But Tomfit lay there, white and stark, with red froth at the corners of his lips.

A dozen men, lamp in hand, came eagerly forward, but there was no time for an explanation. Tomfit was huddled up in garments hastily stripped from the other men, and a flask forced between his teeth. He was coming back to life now, but obviously was hurt, as the crimson stain on his head proved. Then Gipsy detailed his plan. There was some risk here again, but they were all ready to take it.

Half an hour later the rescued navvies emerged from the dust and darkness into the light of day, and four of them carried the injured man between them. It was no far cry to Gipsy's hut, and there they laid him out for the inspection of the doctor.

"He'll be all right here for the present," he said. "I don't think there is anything very much the matter. I'll come round later in the afternoon, and, if he is no better, then we will get him along as far as the infirmary."

But the doctor did not come back, for the simple reason that there was another nasty business in connection with the falling of a crane higher up the valley, that kept all the medical men available going for some little time, so that perforce Gipsy had to act the part of nurse the rest of the day and through the night. When morning came, Tomlit was sensible and clear again, and Gipsy did not enlighten him as to the information he had vouchsafed during his temporary delirium. On the second day the patient was so much better that Gipsy found himself justified in leaving him to the care of a neighbour's wife. He was going away for a short time on business, he said, and would not be back before the end of the week. As a matter of fact, the drama was developing splendidly, and Gipsy was seeing his way to the creation of a part for himself such as he had previously only dreamt of. Therefore he made a painstaking toilet, he dressed himself in his best suit of pilot cloth, and set out over the hills to walk to the neighbouring town of Prestyn.

On the following Saturday afternoon a magnificent specimen of a car wended its way along the rough road leading to the head of the valley. It was all a-glitter with green varnish and plated lamps and fittings, and as the chauffeur picked his way daintily along, hundreds of astonished eyes became aware of the fact that the little figure with the dark eyes and earrings lounging back in the corner of the car against those luxurious cushions was none other than the man known to local fame as Gipsy. This was astounding enough in itself, but, even as it was, the dramatic possibilities of the situation were by no means exhausted. In the other corner of the car a woman was seated. She was wonderfully fair, hair glittering in the sunshine like spun gold, and eyes of tender blue turned upon Gipsy with a smile of the most friendly interest. She was a rare and dainty vision, clad in some wonderful confection of silk and muslin; the exquisite features were shaded by a large hat, the plumes of which filled every woman looking on with awe and admiration. It was, perhaps, the proudest moment of Gipsy's life, though he did not show it. He waved a condescending hand to a group of his mates, amongst whom was the sceptical Ginger, who gazed upon the unwonted spectacle with something like veneration.

"Strike me! Ain't 'e a little marvel?" he said. "Always up to some of 'is games. Tell yer wot it is, mates, wot 'e was telling us the other night abaht this 'ere Tomfit was gospel. And we was thinking as 'e was a-lying all the time!"

"So 'e were," a listener said. "Didn't 'e tell we as Lidy Ermyntrood was dark—didn't 'e say so—and abaht 'er 'air being like raven's wings? Get on! It's only one of 'is games. The lidy's come to see the boss, and she give Gipsy a lift. An' 'im pretendin' as it's Lidy Ermyntrood!"

"They've gone into 'is 'ut," Ginger said impressively.

This point being conceded in Ginger's favour, the spectators reluctantly went back to work, hoping to hear the end of this remarkable story later on.

Inside the hut, the man called Tomfit lay propped up by a couple of pillows, and looked wearily through the open door into the sunny valley beyond. Then he suddenly sat up in bed and listened like a dog might who hears the first sound of a long-absent master's voice. A shadow fell across the sunshine, and a slender, dainty figure came into the hut, as if she had brought that sunshine with her. She knelt down beside the bed and reached her arms round the neck of the man who was lying there. The blue eyes were full of tears.

"Oh, Phil," she whispered, "how could you? How could you be so dreadfully unkind? You must have known I never meant a word I said. No, don't go away!"

The last words were flung somewhat imperiously over the girl's shoulder towards Gipsy, who was silently stealing out of the hut. He flattered himself that he knew exactly what the dramatic conventions called for in a delicate situation like this. But, on the other hand, he was a man and a dramatist, and did not in the least want to go. Still—

"Can't be done, miss," he said. "In all the best plays wot I ever see, especially in the last act, the 'ero an' 'eroine they 'as the stage to theirselves."

"Oh, you funny little man." The girl laughed through her tears. "Can't you see I don't want you to go? I might never have seen my husband again, if you had not been so kind and sensible. Now, you just sit there and listen to all I have to say. And you pay attention too, Phil. Oh, I'm not angry—I'm far too happy for that—and I dare say you want to know how I found my way here, and how our friend Gipsy discovered me."

"Go on," Tomfit murmured. "I suppose I shall realise everything presently. So you mean to say that Gipsy came all the way down to Devonshire to find you? But I'd no idea that he was aware of your existence. Come, Gispy, old man, how did you find out that my name was Philip Trefusis, and that I had a wife living at Edenhurst, in Devonshire?"

"You let it out the night you got that knock on the 'ead," Gipsy explained. "You was delirious most of the time—told me all sorts of things, you did. Took me for the missus, I expect. You was acting a part—acting it bloomin' well, too. Then I noticed something was wrong, and there'd been some misunderstanding between two lovin' 'earts, so I takes the liberty of 'avin' a squint of that little pocket-book o' yourn. Then I'd got it all proper. There was a play already written! Lor bless yer, guv'nor, I 'adn't the 'eart to leave it unfinished! So I just says nothin' to you, an' off I 'ops into Devonshire, to 'ave it all out with the missus. An' fair and proud she was when I told 'er 'ow you got that crack on yer 'ead. It ain't every woman as can say she's spliced to a real 'ero."

"I've been a fool, Phil," the girl said, "a romantic little idiot. I married you because I loved you, and for no other reason. Then I must go reading some ridiculous book about big, silent men who do things and become Prime Ministers, and all that sort of nonsense; and, because you laughed at me, I was donkey enough to say that you married me for my money, and that you couldn't earn your own living if you wanted. And one word led to another. And then I told you that if you could keep yourself for six months without any help—"

"And I was ass enough to accept the challenge," Trefusis groaned. "So I came down here weeks ago, and I have been navvying ever since. Mind you, I don't think it has done me any harm. I have been a selfish beggar and inclined to take too much for granted. But the money never made any difference, Stella. You know that, don't you?"

"Of course I do," the girl whispered. "I knew it all the time. And now, if our friend Gipsy—"

It was a good fortnight later before the Settlement heard anything further from the main actor in this remarkable episode in Gipsy's career. For one thing, the born playwright had been away. Certain overtures towards advancement in life had been made to him by his new-found friends, but these he had rejected, for the present at any rate. The Settlement was too teeming with life and dramatic possibilities for that.

He dropped into the canteen one evening, and a respectful silence followed his coming—indeed, the silence was so flattering that Gipsy began to speak without any pressure.

"Now, I dare say you coves would like to know all about it," he said. "Well, this 'ere Tomfit—wot 'is real name is Philip Trefusis, Esquire, of Edenhurst, Devonshire—"

"'Ere, what price Lord Algernon?" Ginger asked.

"—An' 'is wife Stella," Gipsy went on.

"'Oo put the kybosh on Lady Ermyntrood?" asked Ginger sternly. "An' wot price the bloomin' lord, eh?"

"And the gal with the raven 'air," another intruder ventured—"the gal from Australia with all the posh?"

"Lor, yer make me tired!" Gipsy said. "Presently you'll all be on yer knees to me, howlin' fer mercy an' broken-'earted because I won't take a sup from any of your pots. Now, it's like this—Philip Trefusis, Esquire, is married to a gel wot 'as tons of the stuff. She's as romantic as she's pretty. An' you blokes know how pretty she is, because you've seen 'er. Well, she can't be content with a 'usband as loves 'er, but she must try an' make 'im go into Parliament, an' so on. Then one word leads to another, an' she accooses 'im of marryin' 'er for 'er money, an' nothin' else. Then she up an' says as 'e's a rotter, an' couldn't do a day's work to save 'is life. 'Oh, that's the game, is it?' says 'e. So 'e slings 'is 'ook an' comes down 'ere, and works amongst us anonomous. Of course, 'e told me all about it, we bein' pals; but I didn't rightly know 'is proper name till 'e gets that crack on the 'ead, an' then I goes through 'is private papers. Then I 'ops off to Devonshire an' puts it all right with the missus. Back she comes 'ere with me, an' there was a reconciliation as ud 'ave made the fortune of the best writer as ever turned out a play for the Surrey Theatre. An' there was all sorts o' nice things said about Gipsy, an', if I likes, I can go down to Devonshire and 'ang my 'at up in the marble 'alls whenever I've a mind. An' that, mates, is about all I'm goin' ter tell yer."

"It's a good story," Ginger said thoughtfully, "but I'm sorry we ain't goin' to 'ear no more abaht Lidy Ermyntrood an' the old earl wot lived in that castle for a thousand years, an' give me black 'air in preference to fair 'air any time. Not as that Mrs. Trefusis wasn't a nice little party. I'm not sayin' anythink against 'er, mind; but if you'd a-told us the truth in the first case, we'd 'ave been saved a deal o' disappointment."

"Oh, sit on 'is 'ead!" Gipsy cried. "Don't you know as blokes wot write plays as is based on real life 'as to disguise their characters. Never 'eard tell of the law o' libel? Don't know wot libel is? Ginger, from my 'eart I pities yer ! Wot I 'eard was told me under the violet seal o' secrecy. Perhaps yer don't know what that means?"

Ginger sorrowfully admitted that he did not.

"It's a pledge," Gipsy went on. "Though wot violet's got to do with it, I don't know. Still, there yer are. I 'ad to make Mrs. Trefusis into Lidy Ermyntrood, and I 'ad to change the colour of 'er 'air. And my friend Trefusis naturally 'e grows into Lord Algernon. And 'ow could I tell you common chaps, sittin' round 'ere swiggin' beer, all abaht a private quarrel between a swell young chap an' 'is missus? Wot you coves lack is delicacy o' feelin'! An' now I've given you a lesson, p'r'aps you'll lay it to 'eart."

"You're right, Gipsy, old man," Ginger said generously. "As a gentleman, you couldn't 'ave be'aved any other way."

"Wot yer all goin' ter 'ave?" Gipsy said, with the air of a conqueror. "I'm payin' this time,"

OUT OF SEASON

Gipsy accepted the situation with a philosophy none the less sincere because of its embroidery of quaint expletives, in which the little man was a past master. And once the adjectival storm had died away, he began to cast about him, like the artist that he was, for the grain of gold which past experience had told him inevitably lurked in the most barren soil. To begin with, he was up there alone at the headwater of the Gwylt, and there he was likely to remain, so far as he could see, over the Christmas holidays. The spot was a very lonely one—at least three miles from the Settlement—and the task assigned to Gipsy was a responsible one. Not that he was feeling particularly flattered, for he would have much preferred to have spent his Christmas down there with the rest of the boys, had not the powers that be ordered it otherwise.

Consequently, he was there alone at the head of the valley, his habitation a solitary hut, beyond which was a small excavation, in which a certain amount of dynamite was stored.

The Gwylt at this point had a small tributary stream called the Winny, which diverted itself just here and joined the main stream some two miles below, forming in the interval a large irregular island, and it was part of the business of the engineers who were building the great reservoirs to bring the Winny back into its original course, so as to feed the first of the chain of lakes, and through this certain blasting operations were necessary. So Gipsy had been sent up there with the necessary drills and explosives, with the object of removing a small shelf of rock and thus forming a natural waterfall by which the

Winny could flow once more into the main stream. It was technical work in a way, and somewhat slow, but Gipsy was quite competent to undertake it, and when he had a task of this sort on hand, he preferred to take it alone—there was less danger, to begin with. But Gipsy would have been better pleased if the sectional engineer had chosen any other time than Christmas week.

But, at any rate, here he was in this lonely spot, with no house in sight, except a certain old stone residence which Gipsy knew to be the home of Richard Carmichael, perhaps the greatest novelist of this or any other time. Gipsy knew this, of course. More than once he had encountered the genius on his rambles—an old man with a flowing white beard and moustache, a splendid figure of humanity, with a head like a lion and an eye like an eagle. For five-and-twenty years past the famous novelist had lived there, quite apart from the world, with a niece and an only son—himself a literary man—and a small girl, a grand-daughter, with whom Gipsy had already scraped acquaintance.

So far Gipsy could see nothing in the way of likely material for one of his unwritten dramas. All he could see was a lonely valley, the sides of which were heather-clad and dotted here and there with mountain ash and cranberry bushes. Above them, again, rose the high wooded hills, and at Gipsy's feet flowed the waters of the Gwylt, a shallow enough stream at this point, but ending in one pool where there was always a salmon or two to be found—a fact that no one knew better than the little man himself.

It was a crisp winter morning, bright and sunny, with a hoar-frost sparkling on the grass and heather. And Gipsy was all alone there, and likely to be for the next few days. He had just fired one of his charges, and already he had finished a drill for his next cartridge. For a moment he stood there, drinking in the sweetness of the morning and admiring the glory of the landscape, for all these things were not lost upon Gipsy, who had a natural eye for all that was beautiful.

But, all the same, he was a gregarious little man, and pined for the society of his fellow-men and women. The landscape was all very well in its way, but it lacked the human factor, which, to the eye of a dramatist, is a fatal defect. Gipsy sighed as he surveyed this solitude, and knocked the ashes out after a pipe of the peculiarly poisonous tobacco he affected.

"I wonder if Lady Gwendoline will come along this mornin'," he murmured. "It wouldn't be like 'er to miss a day like this."

In Gipsy's case time not being the essence of the contract, and the eye of authority being afar off, he sat down on a stone and lighted a fresh pipe, his eye wandering longingly and lovingly along the river to the deep, silent pool where instinct told him more than one fresh-run salmon lay. From Gipsy's point of view, the formation of a reservoir at this part almost amounted to blasphemy. For once the big dam was complete, and the valley transformed into a lake, there would be no more salmon in the headwaters of the Gwylt, for it would be impossible for the fish to get up to the spawning-beds. Another year, and the Gwylt as a salmon river would cease to exist. What harm could there be, therefore, in making the best of a Heaven-sent opportunity like this? It was close time, of course, and illegal to take salmon, either with a rod or with a net, till the first day of February; but there were high authorities who argued that the season was a month too long at the end and a month too late at the beginning—an argument in which Gipsy, as an expert, cordially coincided. He knew perfectly well that there were clean, fresh-run fish in the dark, shining pool under the shadow of the rowan trees, and that they were as good now as they would be on the first of February; and Gipsy, the born poacher, had made up his mind that one of these fish should find its way to a certain distinguished friend of his, a dramatist of repute, whom he had run against on a never-to-be-forgotten occasion. But all this would keep—there would be plenty of time in the course of the afternoon—and, the pipe of vitriolic tobacco being finished, Gipsy went back to his work again.

He rammed his charge home, filling up the hole with fragments of rock, after which he set his time-fuse going, and retired leisurely in the direction of the hut. He was all alone there; his danger signals were properly set, so that there was no chance of any mishap. A moment later the charge of dynamite exploded, a sullen roar went booming and echoing down the valley. Gipsy strolled leisurely out to see the amount of damage that had been done, and there, just on the edge of the stream, he found something that quickened his pulses and set the blood beating in his head like the roar of muffled drums.

A man lay there on the flat of his back, white-faced and unconscious. There was a nasty wound on the side of his forehead, from which the blood was oozing steadily. Just for a moment it seemed to Gipsy that the man was dead; then he opened his eyes for a moment, and his lips quivered.

He was quite a young man—apparently not more than twenty-five—good-looking in a rugged sort of way, with close-cropped curly hair and a fair moustache. For some little time he lay there absolutely motionless, until Gipsy forced a few drops of crude whisky between his pallid lips, and then he opened his eyes again.

"Was it an earthquake?" the stranger asked.

He struggled to his feet and then collapsed from sheer weakness. Apparently there were no bones broken, and nothing very serious the matter besides the shock and the nasty wound over the stranger's left eye. But Gipsy was familiar with this sort of thing, and he needed no one to tell him that the stranger was sorely in need of attention. By slow degrees he managed to get the wounded man as far as the hut and laid him on the bedstead there.

"Now, you just lie there quietly," he said, "whilst I go up to the house and get assistance. There's no help for it. When I tell that old writin' cove wot's 'appened—"

"What's that?" the stranger demanded. "Are you speaking of Mr. Carmichael? But of course you are, seeing that there is no other house within three miles. Now, listen to me, my friend. I am feeling very queer, and as if I didn't care what happened to me; but, all the same, I can't go up there. Never mind why, but I have the strongest reasons why Mr. Carmichael should not know that I am here—in fact, he mustn't know, or anybody else, for that matter. Are you alone here?"

"Yus," Gipsy replied. "There ain't likely to be anybody 'ere this week. I got a bit of a blastin' job on, an' you was unlucky enough to run into it. D'you mean to say as 'ow you want to stay 'ere? D'you mean as 'ow your identity is to be kep' a dark secret, just the same as if you was 'idin' from justice? Is that the gime?"

A queer smile trembled on the stranger's lips. He did not know it, but he was appealing to Gipsy on his most vulnerable side. Already the little man was scenting a fascinating mystery, already he saw himself hiding this handsome stranger from the bloodhounds of the law. Here, suddenly, the literary desert was blossoming like a rose.

Here, without warning, was drama full-blooded and strong of wing. This, of course, must be the persecuted hero, the falsely-accused son of the old squire, who had escaped from gaol, after he had been convicted for the forgery which was really the work of his wicked and designing cousin. No doubt the heroine and the rest of the characters in this thrilling drama would come along presently. This was Gipsy's way of constructing a drama, and in this particular instance the little man was building a great deal better than he knew. It was nothing to him that the man lying there in the bed did not look in the least like an escaped convict, though, indeed, the shabby Norfolk suit he wore and his threadbare flannel shirt might easily have been looted on the way and exchanged for convict garb. But Gipsy was too grateful to be critical.

"Now, listen to me," the man in the bed said. "You are more or less responsible for my accident, and the least you can do is to give me shelter for a day or two. I shall be all right by the end of the week. And I am used to roughing it; the plainest food will be good enough for me. And no one is to know that I am here—least of all the people at the house yonder. I am quite prepared to pay for all that I have, and to give you a sovereign for yourself; but I rely upon your secrecy. Promise me that you will respect my wishes."

Gipsy was asking nothing better. Here was a situation exactly after his own heart. If there was one thing needed to make his happiness complete, it was a little candour on the stranger's part. But that, no doubt, would come presently. Apart from all this, Gipsy was a kind-hearted and hospitable little soul, and he would have gone out of his way to help the stranger even had there been no possibility hanging to the situation. With something like tenderness he bathed his visitor's head and tied up the wound. He gave him bread and bacon, toasted on the little wood fire in front of the hut, and beer out of his big stone bottle. He produced the deadly tobacco, but this the stranger refused, saying that he had plenty of cigarettes, which he produced from his pocket. But so far he vouchsafed no further information about himself. He appeared to be quite satisfied now that he was safe in the hut, and that no curious person was likely to intrude upon his privacy.

"No, thanks," he said. "There is nothing further you can do for me. Don't let me keep you from your work. And if you want any money, let me know, and I'll give it you."

But so far there was no lack of provisions, and neither was there likely to be for a day or two. Gipsy went back to his work with a heart full of gratitude towards the kindly Fate that had thrown this adventure in his way. Already in his mind he was building up the drama, already he was beginning to feel his way to the great situation which was to bring the hero and heroine together, and conclude the great melodrama with a fitting and appropriate climax. But Gipsy was not blind to the fact that all this largely depended upon the persecuted hero himself. For persecuted heroes are invariably proud, and are almost grotesquely morbid on the subject of suffering their wrongs in silence. Almost invariably the villain is the weak and wicked brother of the heroine, and for her sake the secret of his perfidy must be locked in the breast of the hero, so that the girl of his heart shall not know to what depths her own flesh and blood has descended. This, then, was a problem that Gipsy had to solve, and, until the heroine herself came upon the scene, the plot would have to lag.

Gipsy had charged and fired three shots whilst he was thinking this over, but so far he could not see his way out. He decided to abandon work for the rest of the afternoon, although it was yet barely three o'clock, and seek inspiration along the river in the direction of the salmon pool.

He had hardly reached the spot in question before he was assailed by name, and a small child came down the steep path between the clump of rowan trees. She was a little girl, dressed in some rough homespuns, her long hair was hanging over her shoulders in red confusion, and her slim legs were cased above the knee in big fishing-boots. Her dark eyes were full of audacity and sparkling with mischief. She hailed Gipsy with the familiarity of an old acquaintance, though this was only the third time they had met. But then Gladys Carmichael was no respecter of conventions—indeed, it is improbable that she had ever heard the word. The grand-daughter of the great novelist was entirely superior to that sort of thing, and, incidentally, she was the only creature on earth who was not afraid of that terrible old man. For the rest, she was utterly spoilt without being in the least spoiled, she was a law unto herself, so far absolutely uneducated, and what Richard Carmichael called the "apotheosis of the natural."

In her unconventional way she had made frieNds with Gipsy, and already the two were the firmest comrades. All children gravitated naturally to the little man, the same as all dogs. They knew by instinct that they had a friend in him, and never had that instinct played them false.

"Hello, old man!" the girl said. "I suppose there's nobody about? It's all right, isn't it?"

Gipsy's mouth broadened into a huge grin.

"It's all O.K., Lady Gwendoline," he said. There was no reason why he should call her Lady Gwendoline, except that the child had constituted herself the heroine of a drama, which, however, was quite another story. "It's all serene. Now, if you'll come with me, we'll catch that salmon wot you've set your 'eart upon. But you ain't goin' to do no good with that there rod o' yourn; it ain't big enough.".

"Say not so, Ali Baba," the child replied. "Say not so, or my heart will break! Know you that this rod was given me by the gallant sportsman to whom I was engaged in the days of my youth—I mean the sailor who went down on the bridge of his ship, singing 'God Save the King,' with all his crew accompanying him on their mouth-organs. Or was it the soldier who won the Victoria Cross at the Battle of Waterloo? Upon my soul, it's so long since then that I've almost forgotten!"

Gipsy shook with inward laughter, for in this child he had found a comrade after his own heart.

"I don't want to 'urt the feelin's o' them dead-an'-gone 'eroes?" he said—"them brave boys for whom you cry yerself to sleep on your piller every night. I ain't sayin' as they weren't 'eroes, but they didn't know nothin' about salmon-fishin'. That 'ere rod might do for dace."

"I've just caught three with it now," the child said.

"No use for our gime," Gipsy cried. "You 'ang on 'ere while I goes as far as the 'ut."

Inside the door of the hut the stranger was standing, holding on to the door-post and gazing down the valley with eager and hungry eyes. They seemed to blaze like stars in that dead-white face of his, as if he could see something invisible to his companion. Gipsy stared at him with amazement.

"'Ere, you jest get back on that bed o' yourn," he said. "Wot's the matter?"

"Who was that you were talking to?" the other man asked. "What is that child doing here?"

"Don't you worry abaht that—she ain't likely to come in 'ere. Fond o' children, perhaps, mate?"

"The only things in the world that matter—the salt of the earth! I was wondering—"

The speaker broke off abruptly and, without another word, went back to his bed again. But all this was not lost upon the little man. Here was the real thing, hot to his hand and burning to the touch of the born dramatist. A less practised craftsman would have betrayed himself and ruined the whole situation, but Gipsy avoided a crudity like that. He began to see his way—the path began to lie clear before him. He was back again by the riverside a few minutes later, with a light salmon-rod in his hand and the deadliest bait in the world. It mattered nothing to Gipsy just now that he was poaching. The thing that mattered was that Gladys Carmichael should catch a salmon and take it home proudly for her Christmas dinner. The child opened her eyes wide as she saw the prawn dexterously fixed to the cruel-looking hook.

"This is really poaching!" she cried gleefully.

"Wot do you think?" Gipsy responded. "Besides, I thought that was jest wot we was after."

"I shall love it," the child said. "Wouldn't it be splendid if the keepers came and took us both off to gaol?"

Gipsy shuddered. This was the only thing that the little man was afraid of. But he argued that it mattered nothing now, because within a year or so the spawning-beds would be spoilt, and the headwaters of the Gwylt closed to the salmon for all time. So he fixed his prawn—most illicit and deadly of bait—and showed the child how to make her cast. A quarter of an hour later, and a fresh-run fish of about nine pounds lay gasping on the gravel before the delighted eyes of the child. It was some little time before she came down to the level of the commonplace again and began to take an interest in mundane things. She sat on a stone with her hands clasped round her knees, regarding her prize with delighted eyes.

"This ought to make a jolly Christmas for you," Gipsy said.

"We don't have any now," the child sighed. "There ain't no high-toned fixings to our Yuletide procession in these days— no, sir. And you can just gamble on that."

"Eh, what?" the astonished Gipsy grunted. "Where did you get all that from? Real Yankee talk that is."

Gladys proceeded to explain. A day or two before, a choice selection of Boston literary pilgrims had come from America to worship at the shrine of The Master, and Gladys had been duly presented to the deputation. She absorbed phrase and accent as one drop of water absorbs another, and the Western metaphor had strangely appealed to her. She was a constant source of surprise and delight to Gipsy. In some respects she was woefully ignorant and simple, but from her illustrious grandfather she had imbibed certain scraps of high philosophy and a fund of quotations, which she used on every available occasion without in the least appreciating their meanings.

"I got that from the Boston pilgrims," she said. "The day after they came I was American all the time. But I was telling you all about our Christmases. We don't get any more since Uncle Basil went away."

"An' 'oo might 'e be, lidy?" Gipsy asked.

"The only son of The Master," the child said. "My dead mother's only brother. Before he went away, our Christmas was the real thing. It's all different now. But, if you like, I will tell you the story of The Great Tragedy."

"Go on," Gipsy said. "I like stories."

"Well, it was like this. There was Uncle Basil and Aunt Lily, who really isn't an aunt, you know, but she's a dear, and I love her. And so did Uncle Basil. Uncle Basil is going to be a dramatist some day, though the only play he has written so far was a failure. It is a beautiful play, but the people in London didn't like it, and they took it off. Now, The Master, he is a funny man, and after Uncle Basil came down from Oxford, he was told that he would have no more money, till his father died, unless he earned it himself. That's one of The Master's little idi-idi-idiosyncrasies."

"Wot's that?" Gipsy asked. "Sounds a powerful word."

"Well, it's what you call a fad. But Uncle Basil wasn't kicking, because he's clever, too, so he just sat down and, wrote that play. And he asked The Master to lend him a thousand pounds to produce it, and The Master, he said 'Rats!' He took an awful lot of words to say 'Rats,' but that's what it came to. And then, somehow, the thousand pounds of his money that The Master had got from his bank, to pay to a builder here, disappeared from the safe, and The Master said that Uncle Basil had stolen it to produce his play. Otherwise he wanted to know who was paying the people in London. And Uncle Basil refused to say. And so he was kicked out of the house like a prodigal son, and from that day to this, which is two years ago, we have never had a word from him. Auntie Lil thinks that he went to Australia after the failure of the play, and that he will come back some clay, when he has made his fortune."

"'Ere, 'old on a minute," Gipsy said thoughtfully. "You are gettin' it all wrong. O' course, the old 'un acted in the right way. Wot I mean to say is, 'e's the sort o' father, the 'ot-'eaded old cove wot's always down on the 'ero, an' finds 'is mistake out afterwards. But you ain't goin' to tell me as the 'eroine—by which I means your Aunt Lil—actually believed as 'er young man collared the dollars."

"Of course she didn't," the child cried indignantly. "She loved him to distraction—I think that's the right word—and she has mourned him ever since."

"An' 'oo did tike them dollars?" Gipsy asked.

"I was just coming to that," the child said. "You see, Aunt Lily had a brother George, who was The Master's private secretary, and it was he who stole the money. We only found that out a few months ago, just before Uncle George died, but it's my belief that Uncle Basil knew it all along."

"O' course 'e did," Gipsy cried. "An' 'e didn't say nothin', so as to spare the 'eroine's feelin's. I suppose you don't 'appen to know who found the money to produce that play."

"Yes, I do," Gladys said. "I know all about it. They think I am ignorant of everything, but you can't keep anything from me when I make up my mind to find it out. It was the lady who played the leading part in my uncle's drama who found the money. She told The Master so in London one day, when he was up there, and when he came back he wasn't half sorry for himself. And he's been advertising for Uncle Basil ever since. Perhaps he will come back some day."

Here it all was ready to Gipsy's hand. Once again he held the key of the situation, once more Fate was playing a leading part for him. But Gipsy was too consummate an artist to spoil the picture by that raw haste which the greatest of all playwrights tells us is half-sister to delay.

"This 'ere 'eroine—wot I mean to say your Aunt Lily—an' is she beautiful?" Gipsy asked half wistfully.

"You bet!" the child said. "'Idalian Aphrodite, beautiful, fresh as the foam new bathed in Parthian wells.' She is all my fancy painted her, she is charming, she's divine. And don't you forget it, old man!"

"Where did you get all that from? " Gipsy cried admiringly. "What a thing it is to be a scholard! But never mind that for a moment. Now, I suppose, as Aunt Lily is fond o' you, I suppose she'll do most anything you ask 'er?"

Miss Carmichael winked knowingly.

"Well, I should smile," she said. "I guess I can twist her round my little finger any time I want to."

"That's good," Gipsy said. "Now, what you've got to do is this. The day after to-morrow's Christmas Eve. You bring the lidy down 'ere an' tell 'er all about me an' my 'ut. Tell 'er— No, you needn't do that. You bring the lidy 'ere an' leave me to do the rest. Abaht 'arf-past three the day after to-morrow. An' I give you my word for it as I shan't be wastin' 'er time. An' now you trot off to the 'ouse an' take that fish with you. Unless I am mistaken, we're approaching the crisis of the drama. An don't you go askin' too many questions, an don't you be gettin' to know too much."

"Mum's the word," Gladys said, and vanished.

Gipsy sat there smoking the pungent tobacco, and watched her till the little trim figure vanished between the rowan trees. He had much food for thought as he reclined there in the winter sunshine, and, on the whole, this was by no means the most unhappy moment of his life. For before his delighted eyes this wonderful new drama was shaping itself. Here was absolutely everything to his hand. Had he evolved the whole thing out of his inner consciousness, the scheme had been no more perfect. For here was the hero, the misjudged and maligned hero, driven from the home of his fathers and falsely accused of a crime which another had committed, and that other no less than the same flesh and blood as the lovely heroine. Gipsy had seen the man who was known to countless thousands as The Master, and no finer specimen of the harsh parent could be imagined. In Gipsy's mind's eye he could see that leonine, head bent in silent grief, he could see the stern lips which had never smiled again. Many a time and oft had Gipsy revelled in this kind of thing from the gallery of some transpontine theatre, many a time had he reconstructed the mimicry of emotion for his own delectation.

And here he was once more the veritable god in the car, pulling the strings of Fate whilst his puppets danced to the tune that he played. He was particularly proud, too, of the child, who, in his opinion, was something quite new in connection with the legitimate drama.

He sat there till the light began to fade and the sun slid down behind the shoulder of the hills. So far the first three acts were all right, but the last and the greatest was yet to come. Gipsy had pretty well shaped it in his mind as he walked back to the hut and closed the door against the winter night. He lighted the lamp presently and made up the fire. Then he proceeded in his clever way to cook the supper for himself and his guest, by which time they were quite on friendly terms.

When Gipsy liked, he had a plausible way with him, to say nothing of a certain innate sympathy, and before he slept that night his guest had confirmed practically everything that the child had said, though it hardly needed this to tell Gipsy that he was entertaining Basil Carmichaei under his humble roof. And he knew, too, that the young man was quite innocent of recent events, and that he had come down there, not with any intention of seeking reconciliation with his family, but merely to have a look at his old home for the last time before it was submerged beneath the waters of the Gwylt. He had spoken without heat or bitterness; it was only when he alluded to the child that the yearning look came into his eyes and his voice grew less steady. Gipsy closed the discussion presently and put out the light. He was afraid lest he might say too much.

"Well, good night, mate," he said. "An' don't you worry. Somethin' tells me as it'll all come right in the end."

It was about half-past three the following afternoon that a tall and gracious lady, with a wistful expression and a pair of glorious grey eyes, made the acquaintance of Gladys's latest friend. She had to be told, of course, the story of the friendship, and how the salmon had been caught, and after that Gipsy expressed a hope that the lady would so far honour him as to have tea in his hut, a suggestion which was received in the most gracious and friendly spirit.

Now, Gipsy had been lying awake half the night, wondering how he was going to lead up to this perfect climax; and when the time came, all he could do was to usher Miss Carmichael into the hut, with a curt intimation to his guest that here was a lady who wanted to see him. It was not a bit like what Gipsy had expected; he knew that he was making a hash of it, and that a perfect situation had suddenly become trite and commonplace.

"'Ere's a lidy as wants to see yer," he said.

Basil Carmichael had risen from his bed, conscious only of the slim figure that stood before him. Gipsy heard the broken cry that came from the girl's lips, then he made a grab for the hand of the child by his side, and dragged her, loudly protesting, from the hut. Indeed, in subsequent calmer moments, Gipsy judged, from the sore state of his shins, that he had been the victim of a bad case of assault and lattery.

"Liter on, Lady Gwendoline," he said. "I don't know no Latin an' Greek, like you, but I know somethin' o' the drama, an' you an' me, though we are 'umble instruments, ain't wanted in this scene. But we'll come in presently."

It was half an hour or more before Gipsy deemed it expedient to knock gently on the door of the hut. And then for some time afterwards he found himself dazzlingly in the limelight. It was easy to see that the atmosphere had cleared, and that the whole story had been told. But to the suggestion that Gipsy should accompany the rest of the party up to the house, and personally receive the thanks of The Master, the little man turned a deaf ear. His own natural delicacy told him that he would be distinctly out of place up there.

"But I'd like to come up to-morrow," he said. "It's a bit lonely for a bloke to be all alone on Christmas Day. An' if I might come up after dinner an' drink a glass of sherry wine to the 'ealth o' all the lidies an' gentlemen, why, if I might make so bold—"

The girl with the grey eyes held out her hand to Gipsy, who took it as if it were something rare and precious.

"You will come and dine with us," she said. "We shouldn't be happy without you. And you must not be afraid of Mr. Carmichael. He is really one of the kindest and best of men, and the humour of the situation will appeal to him. Come up about half-past six or a quarter to seven."

"And I'll be at the gate to meet you!" Gladys cried.

She was as good as her word. And it was Gladys who conceived the great idea of rigging out Gipsy in an old dress-suit of the butler's. And it was Gipsy who sat in the drawing-room most of the evening, with a huge cigar in his mouth, telling Gladys stories of flood and field, whilst the others listened, and The Master, himself strangely and wonderfully younger, conceived the idea of a new character for a book he was contemplating. And, had Gipsy but known it, he was on the way to immortality.

It was nearly midnight before the little man turned his back upon the most glorious day of his life, and made his way back to his lonely hut again.

"I never lived before," he told himself. "I'll tell you what it is, my boy, that is the real thing—so real that I ain't goin' to say nothin' abaht it. I can stand a joke as well as most men, but there's some things as don't bear laughing at—things wot's in a way sacred, if I got 'old o' the right word, an' this is one o' them. But there's one matter as puzzles me. When them two young people gets married, shall I 'ave to send them a wedding present, or will they 'ave to give me one?"

And, with this problem uppermost in his mind, Gipsy turned over between his blankets and went to sleep.

FRED M WHITE – A CONCISE BIBLIOGRAPHY

NOVELS (A-Z)

Ambition's Slave (1916)
The Argus Eye (1919)
Blackmail (1902)
The Blue Daffodil (1934)
The Brand Of Silence (1911)
A Broken Memory (1929)
The Bubble Reputation (1908)
By Order Of The League (1886)
The Cardinal Moth aka The Accused Orchid (1903)
The Case For the Crown (1918)
Claxton's Mill (1912)
A Clue In Wax (1930)

The Corner House (1905)
The Councillors of Falconhoe (1922)
Craven Fortune (1904)
A Crime On Canvas (1909)
The Crimson Blind (US title: The Mystery Of The Crimson Blind) (1905)
A Daughter Of Israel (1892)
The Day: Or The Passing Of A Throne (1914)
A Deal In Letters (1923)
The Devil's Advocate (1924)
Dropped From The Fast Express, or A Daughter's Sacrifice (1911)
The Edge Of The Sword (1907)
The Ends Of Justice (1906)
A Fatal Dose (aka Behind the Mask) (1907)
The Fight For The Child (1925)
The Five Knots (1907)
"Found Dead" (1930)
The Four Fingers (US title: The Mystery Of The Four Fingers) (1907)
A Front Of Brass (1910)
The Garden O' Dreams (1909)
A Golden Argosy (1886)
The Golden Bat (1924)
The Golden Rose (1909)
The Green Bungalow (1923)
The Grey Woman (aka Sinister House) (1928)
The Happy Exile (1920)
A Harbour Of Refuge (1918)
Hard Pressed (1910)
The Honour Of His House (1920)
The House Of Mammon (1913)
A House Of Sorrows (1911)
The House Of The Schemers (1906)
The House On The River (1925)
In Trust (1892)
Jim Crowshaw's Mary (1911)
The King Diamond (1927)
Lady Clara (1913)
Lady Edna's Awakening (1920)
The Lady In Blue (1915)
The Law Of The Land (1906)
The Leopard's Spots (1920)
The Lonely Bride (aka The White Bride) (1907)
The Lord Of The Manor (1907)
Love, The Foe (1910)
A Maker of Millions (1909)
The Man Called Gilray (1911)
The Man Who Found Christmas (a novelette) (1915)
The Man Who Knew (1932)
The Man Who Was Two (1921)

The Man With The Vandyk Beard (1925)
The Midnight Guest: A Detective Story (1907)
A Mummer's Throne (1910)
My Lady Bountiful (1905)
The Mystery Of Crocksands (1923)
The Mystery Of The Ravenspurs (aka The Black Valley) (1911)
The Mystery Of Room 75 (1922)
Naboth's Vineyard (1889)
The Nether Millstone (1906)
Netta, The Story Of Sin (1909)
New Century Calendar Clue (1948)
Number Thirteen (1914)
The Old Secretaire: A Christmas Story (novelette) (1887)
On The Night Express (1930)
The Open Door (1907)
Paul Quentin (1908)
Paul, The Sage (1910)
The Phantom Car (1929)
Powers Of Darkness (1912)
The Price Of Silence (1925)
The Psalm Stone (1905)
Queen Of Hearts (1930)
A Queen Of The Stage (1908)
The Riddle Of The Rail (1926)
The Robe Of Lucifer (1896)
A Royal Wrong (1913)
The Salt Of The Earth (1918)
The Scales Of Justice (1908)
Secret Of The River (1934)
The Secret Of The Sands (1911)
A Secret Service (1913)
The Seed Of Empire (1916)
The Sentence Of The Court (1913)
A Shadowed Love (1905)
The Shadow Of The Dead Hand (1926)
The Silver Stream (novelette)
The Slave Of Silence (1906)
A Society Jezebel (1917)
The Sundial (1908)
Tregarthen's Wife: A Cornish Story (1901)
The Turn Of The Tide (1923)
The Weight Of The Crown (1904)
The White Battalions (1900)
The White Bride (aka The Lonely Bride) (1910)
The White Glove (1910)
The Wings Of Victory (1919)
The Yellow Face (1906)

THE MASTER CRIMINAL (1897-1898)

A series of 12 short stories featuring Felix Gryde, who describes himself as "a really clever soldier of fortune."

The Head Of The Caesars
At Windsor
The Silverpool Cup
The "Morrison Raid" Indemnity
Cleopatra's Robe
The Rosy Cross
The Death Of The President
The Cradlestone Oil Mills
Redburn Castle
"Crysoline Limited"
The Loss Of The "Eastern Empress"
General Marcos

THE LAST OF THE BORGIAS (1898)

A series of stories featuring Professor Victor Colonna, a vigilante physician who murders undesirable people with undetectable poisons.

The Scrip of Death
The Crimson Streak
The Holy Rose
The Saving Of Serena
The Varteg Necklace
The Three Carnations

DRENTON DENN - SPECIAL COMMISSIONER

Drenton Denn is a tough newspaper reporter on the payroll of The New York Post. His hallmarks are a straw hat, a Norfolk jacket, a perennial cigar, and a terrier by the name of "Prince."

The Yellow Moth
The Red Speck
Dust
The Fire Bugs
The Great White Moth

THE ROMANCE OF THE SECRET SERVICE FUND (1900)

This series features Newton Moore, the top agent at The Secret Service Fund.

By Woman's Wit
The Mazaroff Rifle
In The Express
The Almedi Concession
The Other Side Of The Chess Board
Three Of Them

THE DOOM OF LONDON

This sci-fi series of six stories describes a variety of catastrophes which ravage London.

The Four White Days
The Four Days' Night
The Dust Of Death
A Bubble Burst
The Invisible Force
The River Of Death

THE SAGE OF TYBURN (1905-1906)

Each of these stories was preceded by the header The Sage Of Tyburn.

No. 1 - The Chronicle Of The Yellow Girl
No. 2 - The Chronicle Of The Blue-Eyed Syndicate
No. 3 - The Chronicle Of The Inconsequent Princess
No. 4 - The Chronicle Of The Elderly Adonis
No. 5 - The Chronicle Of The Libelled Velasquez

THE DRAGON-FLY (1909)

Six stories about an impecunious but brilliant amateur criminologist, entomologist and ornithologist by the name of Horace Daimler. Each of the stories was preceded by the header The Dragon-Fly.

No. 1 - How Horace Daimler Got His Name
No. 2 - The Three Red Rats
No. 3 - [title unknown]
No. 4 - [title unknown]
No. 5 - A [illegible] Crime
No. 6 - The Mirror Over The Fireplace

REAL DRAMA (1909)

A series of stories published under the subtitle "Being Some Leaves From The Notebook Of A Late Theatrical Agent."

His Second Self
An Extra Turn
"Not In The Bill"
The Plagiarist
The Man In Possession
A Pair Of Handcuffs

THE TELEPHONE STAR (1912)

A series of stories about Keith Marrit, a star journalist working for a fictitious newspaper called The Telephone.

No. 1 - The Case Of El Hamid, The Seer
No. 2 - The Case Of The Genuine Counterfeit
No. 3 - The Case Of The Yellow Car
No. 4 - The Case Of Lord Wintercotte
No. 5 - The Case Of The Rusty Nail
No. 6 - The Case Of The One-Eyed Chauffeur

GIPSY TALES (1903-1916)

A series of stories describing the adventures of a wily British navvy with Romany roots, who is known only as "Gipsy." In his fantasies Gipsy portrays himself as a playwright, and tries to stage-manage the dramatis personae and the situations that feature in the stories.

A Matter Of Kindness
A Liberal Education
A Stranger In Bohemia
Drops Of Water
The Unpremeditated Curtain
Mere Details
Out Of Season

THE DIARY OF A LONELY SOUL (1915)

The Diary Of A Lonely Soul - Story 1 [title unknown]
The Diary Of A Lonely Soul - Story 2 [title unknown]
The Diary Of A Lonely Soul - Story 3 [title unknown]
The Diary Of A Lonely Soul - Story 4 [title unknown]

The Diary Of A Lonely Soul - Story 5 [title unknown]

A Call On The Phone
A Captious Critic
The Case For The Prisoner
The Charlatan
A Christmas Bride
A Christmas Deputy
Christmas Cards
The Christmas Carol
A Christmas in Peril
A Christmas Star
The Clock Struck Twelve
The Colonel's Christmas Pudding
Compounding A Felony
The Convict
Coralie And The Pearls
A Corner In Elephants
The Courage Of Despair
Crossed Swords
The Dancing Shadow
The Daughters Of The Moon
A Daughter Of Nature
The Dawnstar
A Deal In Diamonds
Denny
A Derelict In Clover
The Desert Ship
A Dog's Life
The Doll's House
The Dormer Window
A Dose Of Quinine
The Doubting D, or, A Cranky Cryptogram
A Draught Of Life
Early Closing Day
An Eastern Princess
The Eavesdropper
The Ebbing Tide
The Egg Of The Little Auk
The Emsdam Dispatches
The Empty House
An Error Of Judgment
The Evidence For The Prisoner
Excess Profits
An Eye For An Eye
The Eye Of The Camera
The First Stone
The Foil
Forget-Me-Not
For Love's Sake

For Once In A Way
For Value Received
A Foster-Father
Found!
The Fourth Man
Free Labour
A Friendly Call
From Information Received
Full Fathoms Deep
Gabrielle
A Gamble In Love
A Game Of Draughts
A Garden Of Pearls
Gentlemen Of The Jury
The Gates Of Ramshi
The Grey Bat
The Grey Raider
The Guiding Star
The Half-Crown Princess
The Hand Invisible
Hardy's Big Coup
The Heart Of The Anarchist
Heavy Metal
The Heels Of The Dawn
Her Christmas Dawn
His Christmas Gift
His Majesty's Mails
A Hole In The Net
The Hospitallers
Ice In June: A Playwright's Story
Icky Of Oluk Lake
Imperial Preference
In Black And White
In Rosemary Lane
In The Dark
In The Fog
In The Pit
Introducing Mr. Pentsymon
The Joinville Tunnel
Judgment Reserved
Karma
Kindergarten
The Kingmaker's Token
Lady Mary's Bulldog
The Language Of Flowers
The Last Drive
The Law Of The Jungle: A Tale Of Mean Streets
The Leather-Pushin' Private

The Left Hand
The Lesson The Ants Taught
The Livery Of Death
The Lonely Furrow
The Long Arm Of Bronze
Love In Aether
The Luck Of The Game
Made In England
The Man Himself
The Man Who Got Through
The Man Who Rang The Bell
The Man With The Eyeglass
A Masked Battery
The Master's Voice
A Matter Of Habit
'Merica
A Message from the Flood
The Midnight Call
The Missing Blade
The Missing Note
The Mistletoe Bough
Moray The Traitor
More Than Coronets
The Morning Glory
Music Hath Charms
A Musical Treat
The Mystery Of Room Five
Natural Selection
Nerves
The Night Express: The Story Of A Bank Robbery
The Northern Light
Not On The Records
An Object Lesson
The Odds On Zero
One Day With A Working Ant
One Foggy Night
One Of The Old Guard
On Peace Night
The Onus Of The Charge
The Orpheusia
Ostentation
The Other Man's Story
The Pardon
A Parrot Cry
The Path Of Progress
The Pawn And The Rook
Pearls Of Price
Photo By Lesterre

Pictures In The Snow (a Christmas story)
A Place In The Sun
The Platinum Chain
A Popular Novelist
Poste Restante
A Prize Crop
Proof Positive
The Purple Terror
A Queen In Hiding
A Question Of Money
Rachel's Seventh Year
Rawhide Science
The Real Dramatic Touch
A Record Round
Red Petals
Rob Peter—Pay Paul
A Rope Of Snow
Rose Of The Desert
A Royal Bag
The Royal Train
The Salmon Poachers
Santa Anna
A Satisfactory Reference
Saviour From The North
The Second Chapter
Second In The Field
The Shebeeners
A Single Hair
Sir Jeremiah's Big Shoot
Sister Louise
The Sixteenth Chapter
A Sleeping Partner
Sleeping Partner
A Sound In The Night
"Special" To The Telephone
A Stolen Interview
The Straight Game
The Stranger Within The Gate
Sub Rosa
The Substitute
The Superman
The Supreme Test
The Sword Of Justice
A Table Tragedy
The Thirty-Seventh Month
This Little World
A Thrilling Exit
The Throat Of The Wolf

The Ticket
To Be Let Furnished
Treasures Three
The Two Bon-Bons
Two Of Them
The Unbelieving Eye
Unbidden Guests
The Unexpected
An Unrecorded Crime
The Vital Spark
The Vital Spot
War Ribbons
The Waterwitch
The Western Way
When The Moon Set
The White Geranium
The White Spot
White Wings (1922)
The Wings Of Chance (1922)
The Witness (1920)
The World Next Door (1916)

www.ingramcontent.com/pod-product-compliance
Lightning Source LLC
Chambersburg PA
CBHW061454170626
46811CB00004B/1505